On Three... Baby Reed

Katelyn Snyder

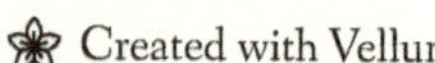 Created with Vellum

To the readers who met Tatum Reed and thought Daddy
This one is for you

Content Warnings

Playlist

i can't help it- JVKE
JUNO- Sabrina Carpenter
Highlights- Sasha Alex Sloan
Wouldn't It Be Nice- The Beach Boys
Gorgeous- Brett Eldredge
Fall Into Me- Forest Blakk
Watermelon Sugar- Harry Styles
Cake By The Ocean- DNCE
Before You Leave Me- Alex Warren
So High School- Taylor Swift
Risk- Gracie Abrams
You Should Probably Leave-Chris Stapleton
The Arsonist- Alec Benjamin
Soak Up The Sun-Sheryl Crow

Prologue - Wedding Season

Darcy ‖ June

Hazel green eyes bore into mine from over Maverick's already shaking shoulders– from watching his daughter toss burnt orange rose petals to the ground as we wait for Kodi to make her way down the aisle. Bella stands beside me with her woven basket, wearing a dress that matches Sin and Harley's sand-colored ones except hers has a giant bow on the back and a baby's breath flower crown sits atop her head. Our best friends are getting married any minute and instead of looking at the flower archway that I painstakingly put together like everyone else, *he* is staring at me. I want to say that I hate it but I don't. Tatum Reed has had my attention since we met at dip night, Kodi warned me that he was my type and she wasn't wrong. His dirty blonde hair is always perfectly swept to the side, and the tailored suits that he lives in are always sculpted to his body and drive me nuts. Continuing to take him in, I wonder what his mustache and five o'clock shadow would feel like between my thighs. Admittedly, we've developed a friendship throughout Mav and Kodi's relationship, but I can't let it go beyond that. Not only could it affect Kodi and Mav's relationship, but Tate and Mav's professional relationship, too. A soft, lyrical version of *Forever and Ever and Always by Ryan Mack* begins to flow out of the speakers and I do my best to focus on my best friend as her Mom walks her down the aisle. Kodi's long black hair is swept up into a bun-braid type situation with gentle curls framing her face, her makeup accentuates her beautiful features but her dress is the star of the show. Her dress is simple yet elegant with its sweep train– its mesh sleeves detailed with flowers and a split front that dons the same detailing of the sleeves. Before she even steps through the archway, Sinclair, Harley, and I burst into tears that don't stop until Kodi is officially Mrs. Maverick Hart.

After the I do's, trying to wrangle the men of the Manta Rays for photos, a delicious dinner of filets covered in a Cognac peppercorn cream sauce, and speeches from the parents— it's my turn to get up and speak on the relationship we are here to celebrate.

Standing from my seat, taking the microphone and one deep breath, I begin speaking, "Hi everyone, for those who don't know me I'm Darcy. Kodi has been my rock and my best friend since we were teenagers. We've been through it all together. The break ups, the makeups, the drama, every nitty gritty detail, so you can imagine that Maverick's proposal was the hardest secret I've ever had to keep from her. She stood by me, boosted me up, and loved me even when I was being stubborn." Feeling the emotions bubbling in my throat, I look at my best friend which was the worst thing I could do because she's dabbing her eyes and that opened the floodgates. I avert my attention to Maverick and

Tatum who both give me encouraging nods to continue, "I'm honored to have gotten to stand by her side today as she married her person. Kodi and Maverick have created a community, bringing people together and giving them a place to always feel welcomed, included, accepted, and loved. To finish off, I'd like to say that my best friend deserves all the love in the world and she's found that with you, Mav. Good luck and thanks for taking her off my hands. Love you both."

Claps, laughter, and sniffles are the melody throughout the rest of the speeches before the party begins.

A few hours later, I'm waiting for my next drink at the open bar, when the smell of the ocean—sea salt and cedar—invades my senses. Turning to look, now aware of Tatum's presence beside me, our elbows touch as he leans over the bar with his order. Whiskey neat—of course, he drinks it straight. "Did you save a dance for me?"

"Oop, sorry. Fresh out of those." I say with more sass than normal. I probably should have held off on the tequila tonight in lieu of Maid of Honor duty but Maverick and Kodi haven't left each other's sides at all and I was sober until the party started. They even disappeared for a little while when everyone was out on the dance floor, presumably to consummate their marriage knowing my best friend and her now husband. I can't help but feel a twinge of jealousy, Mav worships the ground that Kodi walks on. While I date, I have never felt anything close to what Kodi describes feeling with Maverick. She often describes it as if she was missing a piece of herself until Maverick and my niece by proxy entered her life.

"Is anybody home?" Tatum jibes. I must have been lost in my head longer than I thought I was.

"Uh yeah, sorry what did you say?"

"I said that there's no way that you are fresh out of dances." Bumping his elbow into mine again with a smirk.

"You've barely left the dance floor except to get more of that horrific thing in your hand." He adds as he gestures towards my tequila sunrise.

"I could say the same to you, that shit tastes like smoke and wood."

"I'm going to pretend that I'm not insulted by that." His bright, white smile makes an appearance across his annoyingly handsome face. "So about that dance? I think it's like an unspoken wedding rule that the Maid of Honor and Best Man share at least one dance."

"You're not going to take no for an answer are you?"

"You know me so well."

Setting his empty glass down and extending a hand to me, with a sigh I set mine down too and place my hand into his, letting him guide me to the dance floor just as *i can't help it by JVKE* begins to play. I feel Sin and Harley's eyes on us as we walk by them and I can only imagine the comments they are making to each other. When Tatum finds a spot near the center of the floor, he turns to me, places both hands on my waist, and gently pulls me into him. My hands find their place behind his neck as he sways me back and forth. For a moment, I allow myself to enjoy the feeling of our bodies pressed close and his eyes on me.

"You look beautiful tonight, you know," he says, interrupting the silence between us. His eyes, which can't decide if they are more green or brown tonight, find mine.

This morning as we were getting ready I felt like maybe I'd made the wrong choice in dress– the deep V and open back of the burnt orange, floor-length dress making me feel exposed rather than beautiful. All of those doubts flying out the window with this compliment that sets my heart ablaze.

"Thank you. You don't clean up too bad yourself." I smile up at him. "I'm really happy Kodi and Mav found each other. Plus, I think it brought some pretty wonderful people into my life."

"She makes him happy. Until Kodi came into their lives, I hadn't seen him with so much light in his eyes since Arabella said Dada for the first time."

"It's special, for sure." I sigh, feeling the buzz from that last drink kick in. "Do you want what they have?"

His eyebrows raise, my question catching him off guard. Before he can answer, the DJ calls out, "Alright people. This next song is our last one and then we send the Bride and Groom off for their honeymoon! Let's end the night on a high note!"

"Better go and get ready for the bubble exit. Duty calls." I giggle and drag Tatum to the spot by the door we were assigned before he answers. We do a "faux exit" for pictures and then Maverick and Kodi make their final rounds saying goodbye to everyone—spending a little extra time cuddling Bella, their daughter, who won't be joining them on their honeymoon. She'll be staying with Stu, Maverick's dad, while they are gone.

"Byeeee Uncle Tater Tot!" Bella sings from Maverick's arms, her small arm waving wildly at us before Mav passes her over to Stu.

"That's new." I smile in his direction.

"I brought the child tater tots from Sonic one time. So she decided that because tater tots and Tatum sound so similar, that's my new name." His grin grows larger as he waves back to Bella.

"Cute," I say as the DJ begins directing everyone to the doors for the exit.

To my surprise, I can't help but nudge Tate, and say,

"You know, I heard that at these things the Maid of Honor and Best Man are supposed to sleep together."

"Yeah, I think I heard that too." His voice is dark and low in my ear, his body heat close enough that I can feel it but far enough away to avoid suspicion. "Come back to my place?"

Without warning, before I can even respond, he straightens up. Following his gaze, I see Kodi and Mav approach, and disappointment that he no longer holds my undivided attention creeps into my veins.

Absolutely not. I will *not* allow myself to feel disappointed. This is just two friends who have chemistry being drunk and flirty, that's it.

Kodi's arms wrap around us both and she looks at me with a drunk smile and watery eyes. "Darcy, Tate! I love you guys soooo much. Thank you for coming." She hiccups at the end, she had a good time tonight but is going to regret it on her flight tomorrow.

"Love you too babe. Wouldn't miss it for anything. Get some sleep tonight, and send all the pictures," I say, kissing her on the cheek. I reach out for Mav's hand. "Take good care of her for me. Call me if you have trouble getting her dress off—it has so many fucking buttons."

"Thanks, D, I got it off once already though so I think we got it from here." He laughs, throwing a wink in my direction, then prying Kodi off of me and guiding her towards the door. "I need to get her to bed if we are going to make this flight in a few hours. Thank you both!"

I shiver as Tatum and I stand outside waiting for our Uber to arrive. He drapes his suit jacket over my exposed shoulders, and I'm swallowed by his warmth and his cologne. I decide to rest my head on his shoulder, my eyes growing heavy, the business of the day catching up with me.

"Wow," I say, accompanied by a yawn. "I'm tired."

"I bet. You did a lot—It's been a long day."

"Remind me if I ever get married, to just go to the court-house or elope in the mountains."

"Noted." He laughs as a small, blue Corolla pulls up to the curb. Tate double-checks that the license plate matches then opens the door, grabbing my duffel and gesturing for me to get in. To my surprise, when he enters the car, he wraps an arm around my hip, pulling me into his side again. I get comfortable with my head back on his shoulder and eyes closed as the Uber takes us back to Tate's place. A gentle hand nudges me awake and I drag myself out of the car, Tate leading me into a sleek skyscraper and onto an elevator on the opposite side of the lobby, sliding a key card and pressing the penthouse button.

"The penthouse, huh? You are a bachelor," I laugh, letting my head rest against the cool, elevator wall as it begins its ascent.

"I like nice things and pretty views, I can't help it." My cheeks heat when I notice the hungry way he stares at me from across the elevator.

"I do not understand you, Tatum Reed."

"And I don't understand you, Darcy Whitestone." Just then the elevator pings and opens into a short hallway that leads into a sleek yet homey living space.

Tatum drops my duffel by the door and his hands find my waist, spinning me to face him as he backs me into the wall. His lips are so close to mine they almost touch, and his minty breath hitting my face, sends my pulse skyrocketing. His hips have me pinned to the hard surface behind me.

"Tate," I blurt, suddenly feeling like I've downed five shots of espresso—my skin is on fire and my heart is pounding.

"Darcy," he growls in that low, dark tone from earlier in the night. "Do you want this?"

"I do." My voice is faint. I'm nervous because I've always been attracted to Tate and if tonight is the only night that I am courageous enough to give in to our attraction, then I'm going to do this. In a labored whisper, I add, "Just tonight."

"Just tonight."

And then his lips are crashing into mine, nothing about the kiss gentle. He tangles one of his hands in my hair, while the other he has firmly grasped around my hip. I slide my hands up his chest and behind his neck, kissing him until we pull apart—breathless and in need.

"Take me to bed, Tate." I urge.

Lifting me by the waist and wrapping my legs around his hips, he carries me down the hall and sets me gently on my feet. Turning me so he can unzip my dress, Tate lets it fall to the floor before pulling me back to face him.

"Fuck," he groans, having discovered that I wore absolutely nothing under my dress all day. There wasn't a reason to—the dress has built-in support and would show panty lines.

"Your turn, Tater Tot," I say with a smirk. I unbutton his white dress shirt, running my pointed fingernails down his abdomen and through the patch of hair above his pants before popping the button on those too. With a grip on his boxers, he pulls them off and I don't even have time to admire the view before he pushes me backward towards his bed and lays me down, then pushing my knees open. He stops at the end of the bed, scrubbing a hand down his face as he takes me in. I've never had a single look make me so nervous and soaking wet at the same time, the way he is now. On instinct, I snap my thighs closed.

"Don't hide from me. You're fucking gorgeous." He growls, bringing himself to kneel in front of me and pushing my legs open. He leans over me to claim my lips again, before trailing down to my neck, nipping and sucking along the way. His hands roam my body down over the swell of my breasts, down between my legs where his thumb finds my clit and begins to rub in what feels like agonizingly slow circles with just enough pressure that my hips are bucking up to find more friction. "Anxious, are we?" He says into my ear.

"Tate, please." I whimper. Oh my god, this man is making me fucking whimper.

"I like it when you use your manners. Say it again."

God, that shouldn't have been as hot as it was and I am so going to regret saying this would be an only tonight thing. He pushes back onto his haunches, lazily stroking his erection. A bead of precum glistens on the head of his cock. Following my eyes, he swipes at it. Our eyes reconnect and stay locked as he gently rubs it along my bottom lip. Without a second thought, I greedily swipe my tongue out to taste it.

I reach out, and his veiny cock feels hefty and warm in my hand—my pussy throbbing at the thought of the delicious stretch it's about to cause.

"Tatum, please. Fuck me."

"I want you to come for me first, baby." He sinks a finger into me, adding another after a few thrusts while his thumb continues its assault on my clit. I feel his mouth on my nipple, and his tongue swirls around the bud, provoking me; I push my chest up, greedy for more.

"Oh, God." I moan as he finds that spot inside me that is guaranteed to send me over the edge. It takes only a few strokes before I'm a writhing mess, crying out as I spasm and clench around his fingers. And as if this man couldn't get any hotter, he brings his come-soaked fingers to his mouth sucking them in and groaning with my taste on his tongue.

"Fucking delectable, Sweetness. Are you ready for me?" He smirks at me.

"Yes!"

He lines himself up, slowly pushing into me causing us both to groan at the intrusion. Once he's fully seated, he slowly pushes in and out but his bruising grip on my hips tells me that he doesn't want to be this gentle. I move my hand between us to rub my clit and on a breathy exhale say, "Give me more, Tate." That's all the permission he needs, he starts pumping in and out of me at a rapid but steady pace and I move my fingers in time with him.

"You're taking me so well." He groans, moving my hand out of the way to take over. "Fuck you feel so good."

"I'm—fuck—I'm so close, Tate."

"Shit, Darcy, you're squeezing me so tight." There's a sheen of sweat on his golden chest and his movements are becoming more erratic—he's getting close and I want him to let go just as much as he wants me to come undone.

"Tate, come with me."

After a few more rolls of the hip, we both find our release. I cry out his name as he groans into my neck. As we come down, he kisses me gently and carries me into the shower. Once we've dried off and my head is resting on his chest, I succumb to the weight of the day and pass out almost immediately.

The next morning, I wake up before Tatum. If I let myself stay wrapped in his arms, I'll want more and we both agreed that it would be one night only. Before I can change my mind, I carefully unwrap myself from his arms, throwing on the sweats and the t-shirt I had in my duffel, and sneak out before an awkward conversation about what can happen next comes up.

Chapter 1

It Could Let In A Child

Darcy ‖ **6 weeks later, July**

God, I feel like I'm dying. The piece of plain toast I was able to force myself to eat this morning is currently being flushed down my toilet. I feel clammy, and the blue Gatorade I managed to grab in between puking sessions, sits barely touched on the floor beside me. I'm going on twenty-four hours of this and I realize I have to call Sinclair because I refuse to go to a walk-in clinic in these conditions.

"Darcy, baby. What's up?" Her effervescent peppy attitude comes through the phone when she picks up on the second ring.

I'm about to answer but my stomach resumes roiling. "One sec." I mute my phone and heave for what feels like the millionth time.

"Darcy? Hello?"

I hit the unmute button. "Ugh, I'm sorry. I had to barf."

"What's wrong? Do you have a fever? When was the last time you ate?" Nurse Sin has taken over the body of my friend, rattling off questions like I'm running for President and every answer that I give is going to determine if I get her vote or not.

"I don't know, but I need you to come fix me. No fever, at least I don't think so. I don't have a thermometer. I tried a piece of toast this morning but almost everything I've eaten or drank in the past day has not stayed down."

"I'll be there soon. Drink something, preferably with electrolytes."

"Thank you."

She hangs up the phone and I make myself comfortable on my bathroom floor, letting my eyes fall closed. My best friends all have keys to my apartment so if I fall asleep, Sin will be able to let herself in.

Sure enough, I wake up to a gentle hand rubbing circles on my back, and when I crack my eyes open. I am not only greeted by Sin but also by Harley and Kodi.

"Why is everyone here?" I groan.

"Well, in case these come back positive." Sin drops a white and pink box in front of me, pregnancy tests.

"That's funny, Sin. I just have the flu, and because you're the nurse friend, I knew you could bring me all the remedies to make me feel better."

"Have you had a cough, fever, sweats, runny nose, sore throat?" She adds. "Body aches, nausea, fatigue, migraines?"

"Ummm, no." I think about it. "I had some nausea last week, but I thought Harls and I had bad sushi. I've been pretty tired, too, but I blamed that on being burnt out from work."

"When did you have your last period?" Kodi asks gently from beside Sin.

I scramble for my phone, opening my period tracking app, and panicking because I think they might be right. I *should* have had a period recently. The last one was right before the wedding. Looking down at my tracking app, my period was due just over two weeks ago.

Shit.

Fuck.

Oh no.

They don't know that I slept with Tatum, and there's been no one since. I *cannot* be pregnant, and if I am, this tiny human *cannot* be Tatum's. This is a disaster, and despite my dehydrated state, tears are now spilling down my face like a dam broke.

"Darcy—hey—what is it?" Harley asks, placing a hand on my knee. I turn my phone screen towards the three of them because all of my words are stuck in my throat.

"You gotta pee on the stick, babe." Sin prods, already opening the box and getting a little set up with a plastic cup and the test ready for me on the side of my vanity.

"Do you want us to stay, or go?" Kodi asks.

"Stay, please," I say, sniffling. I lift myself off the ground to sit on the toilet. Once the cup is semi-full and my hands are thoroughly cleaned because aiming is harder than it looks, we dip the stick as instructed. Then we sit and wait those three dreadful minutes in silence until the timer we set on Sin's phone starts going off.

"Alright, the moment of truth. Who's looking?" Sin asks.

"Kodi." I groan looking towards my best friend who is spinning her fidget ring like crazy.

"Oh no, no thank you. I think Sin should look, she's the nurse and looks at these all the time." She rapidly says.

"I work in a children's unit, I do not look at these all the time." Sin butts in.

"Ko, please. I need you to do this for me." I interrupt before Kodi can say anything in response to Sinclair.

"Ugh, okay, fine." She gets up, turns the test over, and looks at it. Time slows down as she shouts, "Holy shit! Darcy, you're pregnant!"

A collective gasp echoes across my bathroom and I bolt upright to look over her shoulder and sure enough, the little screen says "Pregnant".

"Oh my god. This cannot be happening." And I'm crying again. What the fuck is wrong with me? I never cry like this, when my childhood dog passed away, I was sad, sure, but I didn't bawl like I am right now. Oh, wait, I'm pregnant by a man I have only seen at two dinners since we've slept together so these tears are totally fine and valid. My mom would be planning a wedding if she knew about this. Oh my god, I'm going to have to tell my mom—she's going to be livid. This will be the icing on top of the cake of disappointment that is me being her daughter. "I need to take another one. That one is wrong."

Sin slides over four more tests and I pee on every single one of them, at one point begging someone to go and buy more—which is quickly shot down. When they all say pregnant, there's no use trying to deny five positive pregnancy tests.

"Maybe we should go sit on the couch and talk." Harley gently suggests, ever the *almost* licensed mental health counselor. "I love you, Darcy, but it reeks like vomit in here." We move into the living room, Kodi stopping to light a candle on the way out.

"So how the fuck did this happen?" Sin as always is getting right down to business.

I don't even know where to start. They know I haven't been on a date or hooked up with anyone in a while, except for Tatum—one I was going to take to the grave.

"Well, you remember how Kodi got married, right?" I open, wearing a sheepish grin.

"Uh yeah. We were all there," Kodi says with a laugh, wiggling the fingers of her left hand, her ring brightly shining at us.

"Duh." I laugh nervously. "Well, have you ever heard the jokes that the bridesmaids and groomsmen should sleep together at a wedding? Like more specifically the Maid of Honor and Best Man?"

"No." Kodi is staring at me shellshocked.

"Fucking." Sin's eyebrows might as well be part of her hairline.

"Way." Harley is so red, I can't tell if she's embarrassed, angry, or confused.

"Tatum was being flirty, and we were having fun that night. We took an Uber back to his place, and I maybe fell into his bed..." I pause. "And his dick maybe fell inside me after he fingered me into oblivion."

"Darcy Marie Whitestone!" Kodi practically squeals. "You slept with Tatum, didn't tell us, didn't use protection, and are now pregnant with his child?!"

"Yes, that is exactly what happened." I sigh, dropping my head into my hands. "It was *supposed* to just be a one-night thing and I swear that it has been. I've only seen him at the family dinners we've had since then."

"You didn't use a condom?" Sin questions. I think back on that night and honestly, I can't remember it even being a suggestion. I don't bother using my words, just shake my head back and forth.

"What were you thinking Darcy? You're like the most level-headed one out of us all." Harley asks.

"For the first time in a long time, I felt wanted and beautiful and confident. I was thinking that Tatum is fucking hot and exactly my type." I laugh in disbelief. "And now I'm thinking that Kodi was right when she said that he and I needed to stay away from each other."

"What are you going to do?" Sin asks.

"I'm not sure. Maybe I need to have Tatum come over, and we have to figure that out together. Can you guys hang out? I'll call him, and then we can watch Twilight while I eat crackers and Gatorade for dinner."

I get confident head nods from all of my friends as I pull up Tates contact in my phone.

"I brought some food that I hope you can keep down, but yes." Sin says. "And wine, but for the three not-pregnant people in the room."

He picks up on the last ring, sounding out of breath. I can hear weights clinking and grunts in the background. "Darcy, what's up?"

"Tate, we need to talk."

"Everything okay?"

"To be determined."

"That's ominous, but okay." He sounds a little uneasy and I hate that I am the cause of that feeling but I'd feel worse if I just blurted out that he is the father of a child he probably doesn't want. "I have to put out some fires this afternoon and have some meetings lined up for tomorrow. I could swing by after?"

"That would be great actually. I'll send you my address. Just text me when you're heading over tomorrow."

"Sounds good." I barely hear an exhale on his end of the phone. "Hey, Darcy."

"Yeah, Tate?"

"Whatever is going on in that pretty head of yours, it'll be okay." He says that until he finds out I'm carrying his spawn, we have to decide what steps to take next.

"Thanks, Tate. See you tomorrow." I hang up the phone and cuddle in with my best friends, but I barely make it through the first movie before I pass out. I wake up a few hours later and find myself alone with a few texts in the group chat.

SIN

> You passed out and you need the rest. Gatorades are in the fridge, the candle was blown out, and the toilet was cleaned. Call your doctor in the morning and us if you need anything else. Love you to the moon and back.

HARLEY

> I'm off so if the conversation with Tate doesn't go well, call me! Lots of love.

KODI

> The guys have an out-of-state game that we leave for the day after tomorrow but call if you need to talk. Love you guys most.

ME

> Thanks, babes! I appreciate all of your support and can't tell you enough how much I love and appreciate you guys. Will update you tomorrow.

I WOULD LOVE to say I'm pacing my apartment waiting for Tate to come by, but I am once again glued to my bathroom floor. I think you'd need a spatula to separate me from it at this point. Through my brain fog, I think I hear some soft taps on my front door. Peeling myself off the floor, quickly brushing my teeth, and doing my best impression of a zombie, I drag myself down the hall to my front door to let Tate inside.

Opening the door, I'm greeted by the man of the hour, looking as if he just came out of a business meeting, not a hair out of place. He also doesn't look miserable, which pisses me off considering his swimmers are the reason I've taken up residence in my bathroom and haven't brushed my hair in three days. As I meet Tate's eyes, I can see him holding back a grimace. I won't hold it against him, he's never seen me in this condition but this is my new form, a pregnant gremlin. He's going to have to get used to it.

"Come on in."

"Darcy, are you sick? I really can't come in if you're contagious. Being sick is not an option right now." He says, retreating a few steps back—a valid fear considering how closely he works with the guys on the team.

"Trust me, Tatum. What's wrong with me is not contagious. Just come in and sit down. Please?" I can feel my exhaustion trying to rear its ugly head and I would love to not be upright. So I add, "Before I pass out."

This lights a fire under his ass, he makes his way to the couch and, after grabbing a Gatorade from the fridge, I sit on the opposite side tucking my legs beneath me.

"So what did you want to talk about?" He asks and I think I can tell that he may be connecting the dots. His leg is bouncing lightly as he waits for me to speak, his eyebrows furrowed and gaze honed on me.

"I don't know how else to tell you this gently, so I'm just going to spit it out." I take in a deep breath attempting to calm the nausea whirling in my gut. The combination of pregnancy sickness and anxiety makes a deathly cocktail. "I'm pregnant, Tatum, and the baby is yours."

Chapter 2

It Definitely Let In A Child

Tatum ‖ July

"**I**'m pregnant, Tatum, and the baby is yours."

Those eight words did *not* just leave Darcy's mouth. My world is spinning on its axis right now. These words, which I never expected to hear from any woman, came out of Darcy Whitestone's mouth—a woman who's invaded my daydreams since I first met her at Maverick and Kodi's. I thought we were just scratching an itch but it would appear that I was scratching so hard that I didn't use a condom. I always make sure to use a condom for this very reason. *I'm a fucking idiot.*

"Tatum, say something." Darcy's light voice saves me from the depths of my mind. "Please say something."

"Are you sure? The baby is definitely mine?"

"Five positive pregnancy tests sure seems pretty definitive." Shit, Jerry Springer couldn't deny five positive pregnancy tests. "I haven't been with anyone since you, and the timeline adds up so, yes. Definitely yours."

"So what do we do now?"

It takes her a moment to answer, biting on her lip as she thinks through her next words. "I don't know, honestly. I haven't thought past telling you I was pregnant."

"Well, do you want to keep the baby? Or did you want to look into your other options like adoption or abortion? I'll support you—whatever you want to do, Darcy."

"I think I want to keep the baby. Tate, we both messed up. I know how you feel about kids. I won't force this on you, but if you choose to be a part of this, I won't ask you to be anything but a father to the kid, and a co-parent to me."

Those last words feel like a punch to the gut. She is offering me an out which is what I thought I was wishing for. But seeing her here, exhausted and on edge, I don't want her to have to do this on her own. I won't.

"No," I state firmly before I've even figured out what to say next. I never thought I wanted to have kids, but something is fluttering deep within me over the idea of raising a child. Over raising *my* child.

"No?" She asks with her brows drawn together, and confusion painted across her face.

"No. I want to be a part of this. Sure, this is not a situation I expected to be in, but I'm not going anywhere. I'm going to take care of you, both of you if you'll let me." I feel so desperate asking her to let me help but I don't understand why. I am *literally* shaking in my boots. Maybe Darcy just gives off an aura of fierce independence and the thought of failing to plead my case terrifies me.

"Tatum. I'm serious, you don't have to."

"I'm going to, Darcy," I reassert. "From now until forever, our child is just as much my responsibility as it is yours. What do we do next?"

"To start with, I need to make an appointment to make sure everything is good. Long term I have to start looking for somewhere with space for a nursery, or at least a crib when they make their arrival." She yawns, and only now do I notice purple bags under her eyes and her unbrushed hair.

"Darcy, you need to rest. Can I do anything for you, should we pick this back up in a little bit?" I feel compelled to offer up my home, but I'm afraid of stressing her out when she's already this exhausted.

"If your demon spawn will let me rest, I will take a nap after you leave. I've barely been eating or sleeping. It's been rough so far. I want to get this all figured out before you leave." She smiles at me, but it doesn't quite reach her oval-shaped, coffee-colored eyes.

"Well, we can take one thing off your plate right now. You don't need to hunt for a new apartment, I have plenty of space in my condo. You and the baby can have your rooms and still be close to me in case either of you needs anything. A break, sleep, ten minutes alone?"

Darcy's eyes drop to her lap immediately. I can feel her rebuttal on the tip of her tongue, so I continue gently. "Come on, Darcy. Let me do this one thing for you both. Those rooms don't do anything right now but collect dust, anyway. It would be nice to have a use for them."

"I don't want to invade your space or cramp your style, Tate. I'm sure you have company regularly." I balk at what she's implying as it couldn't be further from the truth. I haven't been with anyone for a long while before Darcy, and there hasn't been anyone since that night, either.

"Trust me, the only company I have are the guys, and Bella if Mav and Kodi are coming. Just move in, if you hate it, I will help you find a safe space for the baby. If you need some personal space, I have a beach house where you can go if you need to get away from me."

"Okay, you're probably right. It will be easier if we are

all under the same roof, and my lease is ending soon, anyway. Hold on, did you say you have a beach house?" She asks, her eyes lighting up—the first time this whole conversation that dread hasn't been written on her beautiful face.

"I did. You can walk right onto the beach from the back door."

"The beach is my favorite place, my sanctuary. Thank you, Tate, seriously. I would have figured this out on my own, but I'm grateful for your willingness to help and be involved." She smiles at me, genuinely this time, and I feel the urge to pull her into me, but I keep my arms firmly planted by my sides.

"How long do you have left on your lease?"

"I was supposed to sign my renewal next week but if I'm moving out I just need to be out come the first of the month. Maybe we can get the guys together, feed them, and ask for their help with boxes?" She questions as if our friends won't drop everything to help us get her moved in.

"Yes, of course."

"Listen, Tate, I'm really glad you stopped by and we got to talk through everything, but I desperately need to sleep."

"I don't blame you, I should probably get a little more work done anyway. You'll let me know when the first appointment is right?" I stand, and she accompanies me to the front door.

"Absolutely, I want you there." She looks like she wants to say something more, but instead, she just steps forward, wrapping her arms around me as I eagerly return the gesture. The contact helps to soothe some of my inner turmoil about what I've gotten myself into. My dad has always been a great role model for what a father should be and do, but I've never pictured myself in that position. Dad has always done whatever he can to keep our family happy, healthy, and safe. We may not have had all the fancy cars or experiences growing up but we had supportive and loving parents and that's what I hope that I can provide.

"Darcy, I'm here for you," I stress, closing my eyes and lowering my forehead to rest gently on hers. "You need anything at all, make me your first call okay?" I breathe in her scent, just the faintest smell of vanilla remaining from her shower. Unwilling to keep her from resting any longer, I break from our embrace and head out.

Once I'm down to my car, I heave a deep breath and pull out my phone.

ME

911 guys meeting. Now. My place.

MAVERICK

No can do boss man. Bella just went down for her nap and Kodi is out with Sin. Everyone can come over here though.

DOM

Who did you get pregnant?

Oh, Dom buddy are you in for a surprise. I thought it would be him getting someone pregnant unintentionally.

NIK

Finishing up at the gym, be there soon.

COLLINS

Harley and I were supposed to grab coffee but I'll reschedule.

Since when does Collins hang out with Harley by himself? Whatever, I can't manage that circus right now.

ME

Thanks, see y'all soon.

Pulling into Maverick's neighborhood, I'm attempting to rehearse what I will tell the guys, but as soon as I step out of my car and see Maverick's guilt-ridden face, I know that he knows.

"Dude, what the fuck! She told you?" My voice is just above its normal tone so I don't wake up my pseudo-niece as we walk down the hall to the theater room where I know the other guys are waiting.

"Sorry man! It comes with marriage. Any news in the group gets shared between the two of us. I haven't said anything to anyone else, though, so just be prepared." He warns, shrugging sheepishly.

"You're so lucky I'm going to need your help navigating this, otherwise I'd be more pissed."

"It wasn't even me, bro! It was Kodi!"

"Well, I am not going to yell at your wife, man, so you get to take the brunt of it."

As soon as we enter his theater room, all three guys' heads whip up and they are sitting on the edge of their seats. I'm not harboring some international secret—just a small one that is going to change the course of the rest of Darcy's and my lives.

"So who is she?" Dom blurts immediately, and I feel my cheeks redden, a dead giveaway that he's closer than I want to admit.

"You're fucking with us," Collins says.

"Bro, did you not learn from Mav? Always use protection with puck bunnies." Nik chimes in, followed swiftly by a pillow chucked at his head. He's got at least four inches on me, and multiple pounds of muscle, but I suddenly want to punch Nik in the face after his comment. The insinuation that Darcy's a puck bunny has me seeing red.

"First of all, Niklaus," I start, spitting out his full name, "She isn't a bunny. Secondly, you will not talk about the mother of my child like that if you want to keep those precious teeth you're lucky to have left as a goalie. "

"Sheesh, man. I'm sorry," he remits, backing down. Nik isn't one to apologize easily so he must see the anger written across my features.

"Then who is it?" Interjects Dom.

He's so impatient, but I can't shield her from them forever—she's their friend, too. I finally sit with them beside Maverick, who is currently the most level-headed of the group. It's time to rip the bandaid off.

"Darcy," I announce to the room.

"Like Kodi's best friend Darcy?" Collins asks, eyebrows raised.

"Yes, that Darcy."

"Dude, how did this happen? You are always so careful about using protection." Chimes in Maverick, who evidently must not have gotten all the details from Kodi.

"There's always been some flirtation between us. At the wedding drinks were flowing, we shared an Uber home, and now here we are." I explain, choosing not to share the details of my night with Darcy with these vultures; they're as bad as the old women at Baptist churches sometimes.

"So what are y'all going to do?" Nik asks, the combination of his Russian accent and the word y'all stick out like a sore thumb.

"In a couple of weeks, I need all hands on deck to get her moved into my condo. We aren't together, but we will both feel better once we are under a single roof. I'm committed to doing this whole dad thing."

"Wow, okay, another kid in the family. I hope it's a boy." Dom says excitedly. He is such a golden retriever. Ignoring the important details, yet wagging his tail at the prospect of a new pack member.

At that moment, my phone chimes with a text from the Mother of my future child.

DARCY

Appointment is set for the 21st at 2 PM. Figured two weeks would give you time to figure out your schedule. *smiley face emoji*

ME

Yeah that works perfectly, thanks for letting me know.

I pause, briefly, before double-texting.

ME

Please text me if you need anything at all or just want to talk.

Darcy doesn't respond, simply thumbs-upping my message, which stings more than I'd care to admit.

"She send you an update?" Collins asks from across the room.

"Yeah, our first appointment is in two weeks."

"How are you feeling about all of this, man?" Nik asks.

"Honestly, I'm doing okay. Like I don't know if I'm ready to be a dad, by any means, but I don't feel like I'm having a crisis." I sigh. I think weirdly enough, knowing that it's Darcy who I'll be tied to for, at minimum, the next eighteen years soothes some of my anxiety.

Chapter 3

The Blob

Darcy ‖ **8 weeks pregnant, August**

Walking into the OBGYN office with Tatum in tow, nerves have officially set in along with more nausea. The good news is, although I'm not puking *quite that much*—I feel like I am right on the edge about eighty percent of the time.

"You ready to see the little blob we created?" I ask Tatum, attempting to lighten the mood.

"Blob?" Confusion is sprawled across his face.

"Yeah, the baby won't start looking like a baby on these things for weeks. It's essentially just going to look like a blob."

"Let's go meet our blob then." He states as he opens the door to the office for me, a small smile gracing my lips.

"Hello, do you have an appointment?" A small and peppy blonde asks as Tatum and I approach the reception desk. I notice that she looks Tate up and down, which, *how dare she*. Her visual pat down shouldn't bother me, but it does. What if he and I were married or he was my boyfriend?

Clearing my throat, I tell her, "We do. Darcy Whitestone. Birth date, May eighth, nineteen ninety-nine."

"Alright, looks like you're all good to go. A nurse should be out to grab you soon, please have a seat."

"Thank you, we are looking forward to this appointment. First-time parents and all." Tatum pipes up as he guides me away from the desk with a gentle hand on my back. It feels like he wanted the receptionist to think we were together.

"Not interested in the bubbly, young blonde?" I inquire, unsure if I should feel peeved or proud.

"That bubbly, young blonde? No." He chuckles before adding, "Another young, bubbly blonde, maybe."

"What's *that* supposed to mean?" There's no way that I am the blonde he's referring to, so his denial proceeds to rile me up further.

"*That's* for me to know, and you to find out," He responds, as we take a seat in the brown, vinyl chairs that are just wide enough for one person. The waiting room is filled with chatter, and an occasional squeak from our chairs as we try to make ourselves comfortable.

"Hey! We are about to be co-parents. You can't keep secrets from me." I feign offense.

"I didn't say it was a secret, I just said that you would find out... Eventually," Tatum teases, flashing me his perfect ivory smile.

"Darcy." Calls a nurse with bright pink scrubs, introducing herself as Vic.

Another blonde, *because of course*, this time in her mid-thirties. We stand and follow her into a small, sterile room. Vic checks my blood pressure, takes my weight and height, and asks questions about my family, sexual, and cycle history. She then has me pee in a cup down the hall to make sure, for the *sixth freaking time now*, that the pregnancy test comes back positive. I haven't even seen the doctor yet and this appointment has taken a lot out of me. Is this what the next nine months will look like?

Moving on, she guides us to a larger room, hands me a gown, and directs me to strip from the waist down. Once disrobed I can get into the stirrups for the technician to perform the first ultrasound. Vic exits the room, and Tatum turns to the corner of the small space, remaining there until I am settled in.

A light knock comes from outside and a woman named Penny introduces herself and immediately begins explaining how the intravaginal ultrasound will work, asking for confirmation that she can begin.

"I'm ready when you are," I laugh nervously, my fingers rapidly tapping the bed beside me. I should have borrowed one of Kodi's fidget rings for today. From the time that Penny explained how the intravaginal ultrasound worked to right now, my unease has only grown, and I am on the verge of tears. As if he could sense my discomfort, Tate protectively steps closer to the bed, his soothing ocean scent washing over me. "Tate?"

"Yeah, D?"

"Can I hold your hand?" I look into his eyes, my welling eyes betraying just how much I need support from him right now.

"Absolutely." The warmth of his hand engulfs mine, his thumb rubbing over the back of my hand. I hear Penny squeeze some ultrasound gel onto the probe, followed closely by the feeling of the probe being inserted, which is a little uncomfortable at first.

"Alright, ready to see your little one?" Penny pipes up from where she's taken a seat between my legs. A faint bum bump bum bump echoes throughout the room. Looking at Tate one more time for confirmation, he smiles and nods.

"Let's do this," I confirm.

"Ah, there they are," Penny coos, turning the screen so we can all see. I keep my eyes glued to the ultrasound screen as if I can decipher what I'm looking at. The sudden realization I am creating a tiny human within me crashes over me, and tears sting my eyes as I look at the screen, squeezing Tates hand. He mirrors mine with a gentle squeeze, and I find myself tearing my eyes away from the screen to look up at him. His baby blues are focused squarely on the screen, and I don't think he notices me staring as he quickly swipes a tear from his eyes. "I'm going move you to another room and Dr. Freyer should be in shortly after to talk to you about what comes next. It was nice to meet you two, congratulations. I'm sure you'll be seeing me again," Penny says as she cleans me up, covering my legs and stepping out of the room so I can redress.

"Thank you." Tate and I say in unison.

Once I've been moved to the exam room, there's another tap at the door. A middle-aged woman with gray speckled hair enters the room, her laptop clutched to her chest. "Darcy, nice to meet you. I'm Dr. Freyer and it looks like this is our first appointment, where we are just checking to make sure everything is good and getting your care plan established. Am I correct?"

"That is correct."

"And this young man is..."

"Tatum Reed, ma'am. Darcy's co-parent." Tate sticks out a hand to the Doctor's surprise, but she shakes it anyway.

"Firstly, I'd like to congratulate you, cover any concerns, and go over a basic timeline, does that sound good?"

Dr. Freyer explains how our following appointments will go, what foods and activities I should avoid, and ensures that I have prenatals on deck—which Sin, of course, dropped off the day after I got my positive test. When I mention that I've been having issues with nausea and vomiting, she suggests keeping snacks and preggie pops in my purse along with taking a B6 supplement and using Unisom tablets at night. The Unisom is mentioned with the caution of also keeping stool softeners on deck in case it causes constipation.

After stopping at the front desk to schedule our eighteen-week appointment, we head back out to Tates car. My head spins as it comes to me that we won't be coming back anytime soon and the next time we see our blob, they will be partially formed and we will get to find out the gender. Tate jogs ahead and opens the car door for me.

"You don't have to do that, you know?"

"I do, my mom raised a gentleman so get used to it. Ya know?" He winks at me, smirking, and closes the door. Hopping in on the driver's side, he asks, "Is the baby hungry?"

"The blob and Mama are hungry. For breadsticks," I quickly add. "That's what we want."

"Italian it is. I know just the place." He puts the car in drive, music playing softly in the background as he navigates the busy Tampa roads. By the time we make it to Ristorante Bruno, my nausea has kicked up a bit. I need to eat something sooner, rather than later.

"You alright?" Tatum asks when he opens my door, helping me out of the car.

"Ugh. Your spawn is always hungry, and if I don't feed

it, it gets angry." I grimace, trying to keep myself from emptying the contents of my stomach onto this parking lot.

"Well then let's get you something to eat on the double." Tatum flashes me a smile.

I can't help but think the last thing he wants in his life right now is a pregnant woman passing out on him or watching me vomit everywhere. Once inside, it takes almost no time before we are shown to our table, each left with a menu and a roll of silverware.

"So, how are you feeling after the appointment?" I ask Tate as we peruse our menus—I'm debating between lasagna or a minestrone. I don't want to ruin lasagna, my favorite food, if Tate's semen demon doesn't allow me to keep it down.

"You were right. The baby kind of looks like a blob right now. I'm honestly relieved to know that everything is okay so far. You didn't tell me that you were feeling sick all the time though."

"I mean you couldn't do anything. There was no point in telling you." Daring to peek up at him, I notice his eyebrows are furrowed almost in frustration.

"I could have helped. I can bring you things to make sure you are at least hydrated and fed."

"Tate, as much as I appreciate that, Sin is a nurse, and has been coming over probably twice a week to make sure I'm alive and stocked up."

"That's a fair point," he concedes with a light chuckle.

What feels like an eternity later because of my tiny and impatient parasite, the waitress arrives with breadsticks. She takes our orders, leaving us afterward sitting in a comfortable silence.

Clearing his throat, Tate eases the tension. "How are we planning on explaining this to our families?"

Well, I honestly don't know how to answer such a loaded question. I know my family is going to give me the 'I'm not mad, I'm just disappointed look', even though on the inside my Mom is going to be freaking out. I am dreading her inevitable suggestion that Tate and I should marry, and that she's going to spiral into who knows what kind of mood.

"Where'd ya go, D?" Tate speaks again.

"Sorry... I was just thinking that my mother is going to be an absolute basket case when she finds out. When she found out in tenth grade that I had a boyfriend who *wasn't* one of her wealthy friends' sons, I swear she almost gave herself an aneurysm. We dated until right before I started my freshmen year of college and the whole time Mom wouldn't let him attend any events. My parents never missed an opportunity to tell him he wasn't good enough for me on the rare occasion they did see him. He ended up dumping me because he needed more, and I wasn't able to give it while living with my parents. I haven't had a serious relationship since. I mean, I guess we just get my family together and just rip the band-aid off. I don't think we can really prepare them or ourselves for the news." I sigh, continuing my mental spiral around this hypothetical conversation. "Any chance your parents might be more receptive than mine?"

"Well, I'm sorry that she did that to you. That's not fair. No matter how your mom reacts, I'll have your back, Darcy. I don't think my parents are going to be upset, I think they'll just be surprised, which we all were, weren't we?" I don't know if it's his infectious laugh, or the breadsticks delivering their much-demanded nutrients, but I feel my anxiety begin to fade.

"I honest to God thought I had the flu. Then, Sin

showed up with Kodi, Harls and a bag full of pregnancy tests, putting me firmly in my place." I shrug as if it's no big deal. The waitress comes back by dropping our food off. We finish our meal, and I start to find comfort in the silence I've found with Tate.

He drops me back at my apartment, once again reminding me that if I need absolutely anything, at any time, to call him.

Wanting to remove any remaining gel from the ultrasound appointment, I head into my apartment and undress, heading towards my bathroom. In the midst of my shower, a wave of nausea hits hard and I find myself soaking wet and mourning as I heave the very delicious dinner I had with Tate into my toilet. Once my stomach settles, I take Sin's advice, drinking some water and munching on a few saltines before I lie down to sleep hoping that tonight I get some rest.

Chapter 4

Coke Icees Make Everything Better

Tatum ‖ 9 weeks pregnant, August

"She is still in a deep sleep," Sin states, exiting the hallway. "I don't think Darcy got much sleep, based on the way her bathroom reeks and the amount of half-drank liquids she has on her nightstand. Let's get started and I'll wake her closer to us heading to your place."

Sinclair had let herself into Darcy's apartment after our initial knocks were ignored—we have everybody coming over to help Darcy move into my place today.

"You don't think we will wake her with all the movement?"

"No, she's down for the count and needs the rest." We start working in silence until the others arrive.

True to her word, by the time Darcy awakens from her slumber, the only boxes we have left to put in the U Haul are the few in her room.

"Morning, Sunshine." Kodi greets her groggy friend, wrapping her in a hug.

"You missed the gun show." Dom winks at her as he

flexes his biceps, earning a small smile from Darcy, and a glare from me. Luckily, I don't think anyone notices.

"Alright, let's load these last couple boxes and get over to my place for pizza," I say to the room, Darcy begins to move back towards her room. "Absolutely not!" Sin and I both direct towards her at the same time.

"Gee thanks *Mom* and *Dad*. I just need to toss everything I needed last night into my duffel, and pull the sheets off my bed," she deadpans, and I swear I can feel her roll her eyes at us as she heads down the hallway.

"Leave the bag with the boxes!" I yell at her back which earns me a pointed glare before she turns back towards her room.

Maverick, Nik, and Dom hop in the Uhaul and the girls pile into Sin's car, while Collins rides over with me. I expect the car ride with Collins to be quiet but once we are on the road he quickly blurts out, "Tatum, I need your advice. There's this girl I want to take out, and I don't think she is picking up on it."

"Well... have you asked her out?" I sputter, I wasn't ready for Collins, of all people, to confess anything like this to me, but I'm almost one hundred percent sure that he is referring to Harley. They've been hanging out a lot outside of the group and I've overheard the girls talking about how she has this douche of a guy she won't stop going back to. Maybe Collins could be the one to help her move on.

"No, dude, but I take her to dinner, we get coffee, I ask her how her day went. I'm curious if she's picking up on any of this, but I just can't seem to get a read on things." He inhales then exhales. "And I keep all of her favorite snacks and drinks stocked at my house because she's over so often."

"I mean honestly, Collins, it sounds like you are putting

in some effort. You should probably just talk to her, ask her out, right?"

"Well, it doesn't feel so easy. Technically, she has a boyfriend, but he treats her like shit."

The ride to my place is quick, so as we park the car I give him one last piece of advice, "Well man just keep showing her what you can provide. Keep being your best self, and maybe she'll realize how much of a catch you are."

The motivation of pizza and beer, sans Darcy, has everyone moving at top speed to get the boxes up to Darcy's new room.

By the time we get everything up and everyone is fed it's just shy of 8 PM. Bella is passed out on the couch, the guys are watching a hockey game, and the girls are gossiping, but I notice Darcy isn't in the living room with everyone else. I head to her room, finding it empty, when I see that her bathroom door is closed.

I approach and knock gently, wanting to make sure she can find everything she needs. "D?"

"You can come in."

She sounds defeated. I hate that she's having such a hard time adjusting to being pregnant. Knowing there isn't much I can do but willing to try whatever I can to help. Opening the door slowly, I find her sitting on the floor, a wet towel pressed to her forehead.

"Do you need anything?" I ask, gently.

"For your one-night-stand souvenir to let me enjoy food without revolting." She laughs but it's dry and humorless. She's clearly exhausted. While we had plans to let everyone hangout, Darcy's needs are more important, and at this moment I want nothing more than for her to have a quiet home—and some much-needed sleep.

"I'm going to kick everyone out, and then I'll be back to

help you get settled. I'll bring you water with a hydration packet and some saltines on my way back."

"How did you know that's what I needed?" She asks, sullenly staring at her lap.

"Asked Sin what I should stock up on before we got you moved in. The list was exhaustive, but it gives me peace of mind to have it all on hand. I want you to be comfortable here, for this condo to be a refuge for you... and the baby." She finally looks up at me, and I can't help but smile down into her coffee eyes. "Be right back."

Making my way into the living room, I work to get everyone's attention. "Alright, everyone, Mama needs rest and frankly so do I. Thank you for all your help today, take the leftover pizza with you please!"

After herding everyone out, I grab the crackers and drink for Darcy. Finding her in her room, searching through boxes, I notice she has a slight shake in her shoulders.

"Darcy," I start, my voice calm and steady, "talk to me." I approach and cautiously pull her into my arms.

"I don't know where my freaking pajamas are and I'm just so tired, Tate." She whimpers. "I don't want to sleep in my day clothes but I also can't sleep naked. I'm exhausted and my brain isn't cooperating and I just don't know what to do."

"I have an idea, be right back." Disappearing and then hurrying back with one of my t-shirts and a pair of sweats in hand. Darcy is now sitting on the edge of the bed, the shake of her shoulders is gone and the stream of tears has slowed down quite a bit.

"Here ya go, Mama." Leaning down to hand the clothes over, I notice that her cheeks have flushed at this new nickname. "Do you need anything else?"

"Um, yeah, actually."

"Well don't be shy now, spit it out," I tease lightly.

"I need a Coke Icee and McDonalds fries." Glancing at my watch, it's only 9 PM so this should be an easy enough task.

"I'm on it. Take a shower, get comfy, I'll be back."

"Thank you, Tate," she replies, and turns towards the bathroom.

I exit the apartment, hopping into my Porsche and taking off towards the nearest McDonalds. Picking up the fries turned out to be the easy part, finding a Coke Icee at 9 PM was not as straightforward. McDonalds didn't have their frozen cola up and running. I try a 7-11 next, only to find theirs isn't ready yet either. Three gas stations later, I'm stepping back into the apartment with the goods.

I tap softly on the door to Darcy's room, even though it's open.

"Come in!"

Bringing the food in, I find Darcy snuggled in the bed, phone in hand, hair in a messy bun on top of her head, my t-shirt swallowing her small body. My pulse quickens as the sight of her, here and now, sears into my memory. She, the mother of my future child, is gorgeous.

"I'll have you know I traveled to four different gas stations before I found a Coke Icee worthy of you." I bring the bag and drink to the nightstand, setting them down.

"Thank you. Really? You'd think every store had them."

"Nope, four different 7-11's later and here we are." I sit down at the foot of her bed sucking down my own sugary slush. "My mom got back to me, by the way. She's hoping we can come by next Sunday for dinner and then I guess we'll share the news."

"Well I guess sooner is better than later." She continues to munch on her fries as she speaks.

"Have you talked to your parents?" For just the briefest moment, the smile she was wearing falters, but she shakes it off, plastering it back onto her face.

"Dearest old Mother invited me to brunch on Saturday with my new beau." She speaks in a debutante, patronizing tone. "I told her we'd be there."

"Sounds like we've got to wear our Sunday finest and lift our pinkies as we drink tea then." She giggles at my horrible Southern accent trying to match the debutante vibes she gave off previously.

"Yes and do make sure your beau knows which fork to eat his salad with." She lifts her nose in the air as she speaks.

"Wait... which one?" I ask, eliciting more giggles.

I'm enjoying the sound of her laugh as we mock her Mother. Which, admittedly, on one hand is not good considering it doesn't sound like she will be pleased to meet me. But, on the other hand, Darcy doesn't seem to be offended by my little charade.

"Oh no, we're doomed. She'll never accept you now." Her smile stretched across her face before her expression sombers. "I don't know how to prepare you for my parents but they are uppity, Karen-esque and they will view my pregnancy as a scandal."

"Well, Darcy, I will be there to support you no matter how the conversation goes. I meant what I said, I want to be there for you and our little blob."

"Thanks, Tate. I just hope they don't scare you off, I like having you around." She looks mortified that she said the last part out loud, quickly adding, "Having someone to fetch my Coke Icee and all that."

"At your service, ma'am, no need to tip your driver. Get some rest. Goodnight, Mama." I can't help but sneak the nickname in one more time, just to watch her blush.

"Goodnight, Tate."

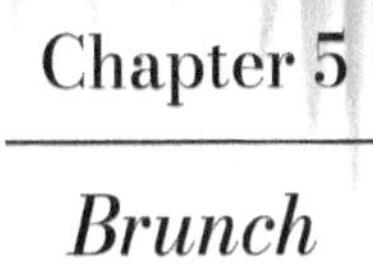

Chapter 5

Brunch

Tatum ‖ 10 weeks pregnant, August

The drive to Darcy's parent's estate is silent, Darcy is radiating anxious energy. Fiddling with the ring I know she stole from Kodi's stash, blowing out a big breath now and again. I want to break the silence, and make her laugh before we enter their home.

"Well darling, it does appear that the weather has held up for our cricket game." I spit out in that horrific accent again, a snort escapes her nose before I continue. "I don't know what's going on in that pretty head of yours, but it'll be okay, D."

"You haven't met Lorraine and Steven Whitestone. If they don't get what they want, they become totally different people. I'm used to it, but I don't want you to have to deal with it."

"You're right, I haven't met them. But, I do know how to respectfully stand up for myself and for the mother of my child." I mean every word I say—she might not be mine, but she is someone that deserves respect and I will continue to back her up.

"Let's get this over with. At least the food will be good," she sighs.

I park the car next to the others lined along the driveway. I jump out, opening her door and helping her out of the car. I let her lead the way up to the front door, walking close enough that her light vanilla scent wafts towards me as we approach the home that gives a particular *old money* vibe. Grandiose white bricks, black shutters flanking many windows and an absence of more modern architectural elements imply this building has been around since the eighteen hundreds.

"Listen I know how this looks but my Mom's favorite movie is *Gone with the Wind* and says this house is an exact replica of one she saw in the movie," Darcy explains. "This isn't a family home passed down for generations. We have wealth... Just, not the kind that is associated with this type of home."

Before I have any chance to respond, the large wooden doors swing open. A woman who looks just like Darcy, but thirty years in the future, awaits, clothed in a pristine floral print dress, a disapproving look, and a ring the size of my eyeball on her left hand. I watch Darcy's shoulders immediately tense as the woman I presume to be her mother pulls her into a hug.

"Hey, Mom." The lack of excitement in Darcy's tone isn't lost on me. She pulls away quickly from her mothers embrace, taking one too many steps backwards, and ends up with her back smooshed against my front. "Oops, sorry."

"It's okay, D. Take a breath," I whisper just loud enough for her to hear before she moves forward, dropping her shoulders back down to a comfortable position. I take this opportunity to step forward with an extended hand, "Mrs. Whitestone."

"You must be Tatum. I'm Lorraine." She takes my hand, visibly inspecting me, probably looking for a wrinkle in my shirt or tattoos which are hidden beneath my pristine blue button up shirt.

"Please, call me Tate. It's a pleasure to meet you, Mrs. Whitestone."

"Okay, Tate. Let's get you both inside, brunch is nearly ready." Lorraine guides us through her home into a dining area where a man with white hair sits, sipping on coffee based on the fragrance. A spread of fruit, pastries, juices, bacon, waffles, eggs and other foods are on the giant spruce table in front of us.

"Darcy, it's about time you joined us," The man says without looking up at us, as if we aren't early.

"Nice to see you too, Father," Darcy forces out. I bite my tongue attempting not to ruin brunch before it's even started.

"Steven, Darcy brought her boyfriend, Tate, with her today." Mrs. Whitestone interjects and he finally looks up meeting my eyes. At this point neither Darcy nor myself has corrected her, but they are definitely in for some news.

"Nice to meet you, sir," I say, as Darcy grabs my hand, pulling me to sit beside her at the table. She doesn't let it go as we sit, squeezing my hand tightly—I don't know if she's doing it for her benefit or mine.

"Pleasure. So, Tatum, what is it that you do for work?" Steven asks.

"Oh we're getting right to business then, I see." I chuckle lightly until it appears I'm the only one in on the joke. "Well sir, I manage PR and schedules for a few players on the Tampa Bay Manta Rays." What they don't know is how I was supposed to be one of those players, but I brush the sour memory aside. Now isn't the time for self pity.

"Fascinating. Our Darcy isn't big on sports, so I'm curious how you two met." Lorraine interrupts.

"Mom, I've already told you that I met him through Kodi and Maverick. Tatum was Mav's best man in their wedding," Darcy recounts with a tight, sterile smile. "And to set the record straight, Tate is not my boyfriend."

"You brought a friend to a family brunch?" Lorraine questions pointedly, like it is out of the question she would bring platonic friends to family events.

"Yes, Mom, I did, and for good reason." Darcy exhales and I know the bandaid is about to be ripped off. I give her hand a reassuring squeeze. "Mom, I'm pregnant, Tatum is the father, and we will be raising our child together, but we're not in a romantic relationship. We're going to co-parent."

"What do you mean you will be co-parenting?" Lorraine gasps. I can see Darcy wrestling to hold back her eye roll.

"It means that even though Darcy and I aren't dating, we both will be involved in our child's life. We're a team," I interject.

"I don't think anyone asked you, son," her father growls, shooting daggers at me with his eyes. I know it isn't ideal for us to not be together, but I didn't expect to be met with hostility when we quite literally are sitting in front of them showing them that we are in this together. Why isn't that enough?

"Well, Dad, that's what we have decided to do. This is our child, end of story."

I squeeze her hand—a silent praise for standing up for herself, and a reminder that I've got her back.

"Are you saying a wedding is entirely out of the question? At any point?" Her mom counters indignantly, I look to Darcy, trying to gauge her reaction. There's undeniably chemistry between us, but I doubt she cares for me in the same manner I've begun to feel for her.

"Mom, let it go. Tatum treats me well." When she says that, a small bloom of hope fires up on the outskirts of the anger that's been simmering since this conversation with her parents began.

If mice existed in this home, you would be able to hear them scurry across the floor as the room seems to fall out of time, an uncomfortable hush filling the space. However, it's short-lived, before Steven's face turns the most ferocious red and he erupts, startling the three of us.

"That is unacceptable Darcy. You can't go and whore yourself out, then bring random men into my home," he booms, "expecting me to welcome them with open arms. You're so selfish, did you, even once, consider how badly this will reflect on our family's reputation? You *will* marry him or you will no longer be welcome in this home or this family."

Beside me, I hear a small whimper and out of the corner of my eye, I see that Darcy has tears running down her cheeks. Lorraine's face is tight, her lips pursed tightly, nodding her head in agreement with her husband. My vision blurs as my better judgement is smothered by rage, boiling up within me, I drop Darcy's hand, squeezing my fists at my side, white-knuckled and shaking, so I don't cross-check this man for disrespecting the mother of my child like that. How could he call his own child such a vile name with no hint of remorse?

I take a deep breath and hold it for just a moment, giving order to the chaos in my brain. In as level of a tone as

I can muster, I let him have it. "You know what? The fact that you aren't even the least bit excited about your new grandchild, and having the gall to call *your own child* a whore tells me everything I need to know about you. You've made it clear to me that I don't want you to have any role in my child's life." Steven glares in response, seething, but I can't find a single fuck to give about what he has going on behind those soulless windows often misunderstood as his eyes. I extend a hand towards Darcy, helping her up and pulling her into my side, my arm protectively wrapped around her shoulder. "Darcy, I think we should go. Your parents clearly don't deserve to be part of our child's life nor do they want to be."

Lorraine follows behind us, desperate to capture our attention as we exit the estate's front doors. She's now a blubbering mess, like she wasn't in blind agreement with her husband's decisions two minutes ago.

"Darcy," she wails between sobs, "Please... you know your daddy doesn't mean any of that!"

I don't slow down as I proceed to walk Darcy to the car, opening her door and closing it behind her. I hop in and peel out of the driveway, placing my hand on Darcy's knee before speaking, "I am so sorry that he said those things to you, he's just an uptight prick. You deserve *better*, Darcy."

She lets out an exasperated, hollow laugh. "That went way worse than I thought it was going to. I..." She sniffles, "I expected them to be upset, expected my Mom to try and start planning a wedding before being sorely disappointed. I didn't expect to be called a whore and disowned."

"Would a Coke Icee make you feel better?" I ask, squeezing her knee gently as I continue back into town towards our place.

"It wouldn't hurt to try it." I catch a small smile in my

periphery. "Do you think it will go better with your parents tomorrow?"

"I know for a fact that it will. But, if you aren't feeling up to it after today, we can reschedule."

"That might be a good idea. I don't want to go into tomorrow feeling so freshly heartbroken."

"Okay, do you mind if I call my mom real quick?" I ask.

"Go ahead, I feel bad. Tell her I'm sorry."

I press call on my mom's contact and her sweet yet calming voice filters through the car speakers. "Hi, Tate. You're on speaker with dad."

"Hey guys, just wanted to call about tomorrow. I'm going to come to dinner alone, Darcy isn't feeling well. Can we reschedule for, let's say, three weeks from today?" I look to Darcy for confirmation and she nods her head at me.

"Oh, I'm sorry she isn't feeling well, but yes, we'd still love to meet her." My mom's empathy radiating through the phone call.

"She's looking forward to it, too, and is sorry to miss tomorrow. I'll still swing by tomorrow night."

"Sounds good, we love you. Send our love to Darcy."

"Will do, love you guys." Then the line goes dead and I see Darcy smile softly from the corner of my eyes, hoping this has helped her feel a little better after the shit show that was today. After securing her Icee, we head home so she can rest.

Chapter 6

Surprise

Darcy || 13 weeks pregnant, September

The night following brunch with my parents I couldn't stop thinking about how Tatum stood up for me. No one has ever stood up to my father like that, and admittedly, it was hot as fuck. Tatum's vein popping as he clenched and unclenched his fist under the table, the protective arm he wrapped around me, and the way he *repeatedly* checked in on me until we got home and I passed out. Now, three weeks later, I'm standing in front of the mirror, noticing how my black yoga pants are hugging my thighs a little tighter and my stomach looks a little swollen. I throw on a light green, oversized flannel that hangs off my shoulders revealing the lace strap of my cream bralette to show off the small wave tattoo that adorns my collarbone. It's a small, but meaningful, reminder of my happy place. My long hair is in a messy braid hanging on my opposite shoulder. I pull my phone out, snapping a pic to show the girls, Ko, Harls, and Sin.

KODI

OMG! A little bump!

ME

I think it's just water weight?

SIN

Might be but it's still cute. Have you been doing monthly photos?

ME

No! Omg, I'm going to start making Tatum take them for me. I mean I'm only thirteen weeks along so we didn't miss too many.

HARLS

Yes! Document this journey. It'll be cool to see how you change and then see the blob outside of the womb.

KODI

You're calling it a blob, too? Ugh.

ME

What else are we supposed to call it? We don't know if it's he or she yet, so blob it is.

"Hey, you about ready?" Tatum's voice causes me to jump.

"How long have you been standing there?"

"Long enough to watch you take a picture of your stomach," he says, stepping into the room, "may I touch it?"

"Um, sure. I don't think you'll feel anything and it's mostly water weight I think."

"That's okay, I just want to say hello to our little blob." He steps closer to me, dropping to his knees in front of me and I'm going to blame the pregnancy hormones for the way my pussy clenches at the sight.

"Kodi still thinks it's weird we are calling it a blob." I laugh as he gently presses a hand to my stomach.

"Hi, little dude or lady. It's your dad here, just saying hello." He speaks directly to my stomach and for some reason it makes me giggle and Tate looks up at me with his brow furrowed, "What?"

"I'm sorry it's not you, this is very sweet, it's just also very weird to me. I think that after the gender appointment they might be able to hear you."

"That's fair, this whole situation is a little weird, isn't it?" He asks me.

"It definitely is. We need to take monthly photos to document my stomach growing, can you take one quick? Then we can go." Tatum pulls his phone out quickly as I stand against the empty wall in my room, facing sideways and letting a small smile grace my face. Then Tatum does something that surprises me, he steps forward and gently lays his left hand back on my stomach snapping another photo before pocketing his phone.

"Thanks, let's get out of here."

WE BARELY MAKE it out of the car before Tatum's mom and seventeen-year-old twin sisters have their arms wrapped around us, squealing that they missed him so much and telling me how beautiful I am.

"She is, isn't she?" Tatum says to them. I've chosen to forgo makeup today, which gives them a clear view of my cheeks flushing at his praise.

"Okay, people, let the woman breathe." Tatum chuckles as they detangle themselves from around us. Up on the porch stands an older, yet still handsome, version of Tatum —his greying hair and numerous crinkles at the corner of his eye stand out to me as he grins at our approach. He wraps Tate in a hug before introducing himself.

"Hi, sweetheart. I'm Walter, this is my wife, Rose, and our daughters, Tessa and Tinsley. I think they forgot to introduce themselves in the excitement of things."

"It's nice to meet you, Walter. I see now where Tate gets his good looks from." They all laugh at this and instantly I feel ten times more comfortable here than I did at my family brunch.

"Any friend of our Tate is welcome here." Rose chimes in, smiling at her husband with so much love and adoration that my heart squeezes inside of my chest. It twinges in a more painful way, when my mind pieces together that Tatum told them ahead of time I am just his friend. I know I shouldn't hope for more and that I'm the one who wanted a one-night stand, but the decision is slowly starting to come back and haunt me.

Following Walter inside, I notice the aura of their home is much different from the one I grew up in. It smells inviting, like freshly baked vanilla cookies. On almost every wall are pictures of family vacations, baby Tatum and his siblings, senior photos from all three kids, and other precious family memories—I can't help but wonder how similar our baby will look compared to Tatum as a child. His hair much lighter, a carefree and lopsided grin on his face, his eyes still bright as ever. To the left of the entryway sits a family room that is, somehow, covered in more family photos. Two small, gray couches sit on opposite sides of a coffee table holding a few board games such as Scrabble and Monopoly. Across from the living room is a dining space, with fresh flowers sitting atop an oakwood table with six place settings. Speaking of food, whatever Rose has cooked up smells like comfort, matching the vibes of these people and this home. We file into the room, Tessa and Tinsley following Rose into the kitchen to help her bring the food to the table, when I offered to help I was told to have a seat because guests don't work in this home.

Ten minutes later, our bowl-shaped plates—the superior kind of plate if I do say so myself—are piled high with pot roast, mashed potatoes, and cornbread. We sit chatting lightly about Tates work and the wedding, enjoying our meals for a few moments before our blob decides that they are not enjoying the meal as much as I thought.

Tate leans in, whispering under his breath, "Are you okay?"

"Nope, bathroom."

"First door on the left."

I'm out of my chair and leaning over the toilet before Tate could say anything else, and I hear him get up to follow me, based on the grating of his chair legs across the floor.

"Sorry, you had to witness that," I sigh. I rinse my mouth in the sink and snag some mouthwash from the cabinet underneath. "We only have eight to ten more weeks of this, at least that's what the internet says to expect... Hopefully."

"I'm sorry, D. You okay to go back in there?"

"Yep." We make our way back to the dining room where everyone else is still eating.

"Darcy, are you okay sweetheart?" Rose asks, her eyes seeming to see right through me; her furrowed eyebrows and pursed lips cluing me in that our blob may not be a secret any longer. Tate pushes my chair back into the table after I've sat. I look up at Tate, attempting to gauge if this is the time to break the news or not. Taking his seat beside me again, he gives me an encouraging nod.

"The food is delicious, Rose, really. I would have liked to eat some more of it. I just... well... I can't..." I sputter, feeling more nervous about sharing the news with Tate's family than my own. Despite feeling welcomed here, I'm still uncomfortable at the idea of just spitting out such big news.

"What Darcy is trying to say," Tate announces, taking over for me, "is that she was enjoying dinner until our child decided that they didn't enjoy it." Tate, in a show of support, moves his chair closer and wraps his arm protectively around me just like he did at family brunch three weeks ago—only this time, it feels more like a comfort rather than a shield.

Simultaneously, Tessa and Tinsley begin squealing about becoming aunties, Walter chokes on his water, and Rose starts to sob.

"Now, before anyone gets too excited," interrupts Tatum, shooting a pointed glare at his sisters that quiets them almost immediately. "We have some important details you all should know. We are not in a romantic relationship, and we might never be. We spent one night together, this," continues Tatum, gesturing towards Blobby, "pregnancy happened, and we decided that we want to raise this child together under one roof as a co-parenting family rather than separately."

"Ew, Tate, you didn't have to spell out that you had sex," Tessa groans, while Tinsley mimes barfing, to my amusement.

"Well, I must say that I am surprised, but still so excited for the both of you. I'm going to be a Gramma," Rose says, batting at some tears. "Regardless of your relationship status, you are now a part of this family, Darcy, and will always be welcome in our home."

My heart pinches in my chest, tears prick the back of my eyes and I feel Tate's hand rubbing circles on my lower back.

"Thank you, your support means so much. Our kid is going to be lucky to have all of you in their life."

"And they will be really lucky to have you both as parents." Walter smiles beside his tearful wife, I can see emotions swimming in his eyes. The happiness, the surprise, the excitement.

With full bellies, and overflowing hearts, we eventually move over to the living room with Tatum and Walter leaving us girls to chat. Rose delves right in, asking me how I'm feeling, how my parents reacted, and a multitude of other questions regarding my life and pregnancy. The twins offer to babysit for a hefty fee, drawing Rose's ire. She wastes no time, telling them that, as aunties, they provide babysitting for the low price of free—it's written into the job description. Eventually the men return, joining us, and we play one very long and very competitive game of Monopoly before Tatum and I have to head out.

The next morning, to our surprise, we open our front door and find a giant box addressed to Tate and me. Within, we discover a plethora of baby clothes, preggy pops, baby bottles, stuffies, and books—along with a note from Rose. Sniffling as I read the note, I am overtaken by the overwhelming amount of love and support given by Tatum's mom.

Darcy and Tatum, I couldn't help myself, I had to start

my Gramma shopping this morning. Once I started, I couldn't stop. Please call me if you can think of anything you need or, Darcy, if you are ever wanting someone to talk to about pregnancy or motherhood with. I love you both, Mama Rose.

Is this what family is supposed to feel like?

Chapter 7

Vitamin D

Darcy ǀ 13 weeks pregnant, September

"So you're telling me that the way he stood up for you to your Dad didn't make you feel any sort of warm, tingles down there?" Kodi asks, crudely gesturing to my crotch. While it absolutely did, I am refusing to admit it. It's been a few days since dinner at the Reed's, and I am finally getting to sit down and talk about the family drama with my best friends. I could've texted them, but this felt like something I needed to talk about in person.

"Nope," I respond, popping the P for added emphasis. Kodi, Sin, Harley, and I decided to have a girl's night, Bella included, where we are enjoying charcuterie and wine—sparkling apple juice for me and Bella, though, before she went to bed for the night. The guys are away for a game, which is, of course, playing quietly in the background.

"Uh-huh. For some reason, I don't believe you," Harley murmurs, smirking down at her phone.

"Okay, Mrs. Secretive. Who's got you smiling like that?" I ask, attempting to change the subject.

"You guys are going to be mad at me," she responds, and I immediately know she's talking to Benji for the fourth time this year. They fuck around together, he does what he calls "at-home date nights" so he doesn't have to take her out in public, and he's always making up some excuse as to why he can't be in a relationship with her—leaving us to pick up the pieces. The boy isn't even anything special, a finance bro taking advantage of our sweet friend over and over again.

"Ugh. Harls, not again." Kodi whines.

"Listen, he's *different* this time. He's already taken me out on a few dates. *In public!* He even picked me up and drove me to them!" Harley cringes at herself, knowing but refusing to accept just how bad it sounds out loud.

"Babes, that is *literally* the bare minimum," Sin sighs. As Harley's roommate, Sin deals with the majority of the fallout he causes. "Promise me that if there is a next time it will be the last time. We can't keep seeing you get hurt like this."

"Yeah, you're right. I promise." She bites her lip apprehensively, and I fear that maybe it won't be the last time—or that he's already making her feel that way. "Okay let's talk about something different. D, when are you going to take Tatum up on the offer to visit the beach house? Collins says it's really beautiful and a picturesque sunset viewing location."

"We are heading out there in a couple of weeks. Work has been killer, and I just need some time away from it all," I groan, thinking about the sand between my toes and the sun beating down on my skin, the ocean washing my worries away with each wave that crashes against the shore.

"Oh so you're getting some Vitamin D. By D, I mean di-." Sin begins.

"No, by Vitamin D, you mean from the sun because that's the only D I'm getting these days—unless it's bright pink and vibrates." I butt in, effectively cutting her off. They all roll their eyes at me as if to say Tatum and I will inevitably end up together.

"D, I hate to tell you this but you and Tate have flirted every time you've been around each other. You're just naturally drawn to one another. Moth to flame and all that." Kodi, my best friend, can say to me whatever she wants, however, she wants, and more often than not it's something annoyingly on the nose or a truth I've been avoiding accepting for too long. "I'm just saying Mav and I denied our attraction to each other until I had to force his hand, dragging Nik into it. Now look at us, in love and shit."

Sin mimes puking while Harley is still engrossed in her phone and I resign myself to the fact that she is probably right. I can continue to deny that Tate and I have chemistry and work well together or, maybe there's a way I can ride the wave and find out if we stay above water or get pulled under.

PULLING up to the beach house late last night, it was the exact opposite of the condo. The exterior is pulled right out of a coastal living magazine, with a light blue exterior and white shutterboard windows. The interior consists of a mostly open floor plan. The kitchen, with marble counters and beige cabinets, leads into a living room holding a white couch covered in blue pillows, and a coffee table made of driftwood sitting in the middle. Tatum shows me to the room I'll be staying in, at the back of the house, housing a queen-sized bed and an en suite. Glass doors lead to the back patio. Spotting a brown wicker swinging egg chair, I decide it makes the perfect location for me to sit and drink my one doctor-permitted coffee before we hit the beach.

"I'll never get tired of the salty air and the crisp sun beating down on my skin." I exhale as I plop down on my beach blanket next to the umbrella Tatum has set up. I close my eyes, leaving my skin to soak up the only Vitamin D that I'll be getting this weekend.

"It is peaceful here," agrees Tate. "Sometimes when I need to get away or think. I just drive out here and sit, no matter the time. The waves crashing against the shore is such a soothing sound."

"I get why babies like sound machines. This sound could put me to sleep right now." I can feel my body beginning to relax—the beach has always been my escape. When my parents left me feeling like I wasn't enough, I would just vamoose to the beach for hours usually with Kodi to decompress.

"Feel free to shower or nap, you don't have to hang out with me all weekend. If you want, we could reconvene for dinner. I have some steaks to grill, a salad, and potatoes being delivered soon."

"Mmm, that sounds delicious." I moan, almost immediately regretting how excited I got over the prospect of a steak. "I think I am going to hit the hay for a bit, see you around five?"

"Perfect, see you soon, Mama," Tate says, smiling at me as I get up and walk away.

Three hours later we are sitting across from each other with cleared plates and sated appetites.

"The blob must have enjoyed dinner because I feel

great," I say almost too enthusiastically. At this point, few foods don't, at minimum, make me nauseous.

Tate's chest puffs with pride, "I'm so glad to hear that, partly because I was going to see if you wanted to join me to watch the sunset. This section of the shoreline is pretty secluded, as you pointed out, so we can just bask in its beauty together."

"I'd like that a lot."

We work simultaneously to clean up from dinner, then grab my beach blanket and head down to the shore. Tate helps me down, quickly joining me on the ground, leaning back on his hands, our legs almost touching. We sit in serene silence for a while just enjoying the view of the cotton candy sky. Silence with Tatum isn't uncomfortable. It's effortless to sit here with him, no words flitting between us. I've only ever experienced this type of calm with Kodi. Not even with my parents have I ever felt this relaxed, tension would always coil in my gut making me feel queasy.

"No matter how many times I do this, the view never grows wearisome." He says as the last rays of sunlight fade, a smooth breeze caressing in the darkness.

"I'd love to live out here one day."

"I always wanted to, you know?"

"Wanted to live on the beach?" I ask as a chill wracks my body.

Without any hesitation, Tate hands me his black Manta Rays hoodie. I pull it over my head, letting his scent and warmth wrap around me.

"Thank you. Seriously, thank you for this weekend, I needed it."

He remains close at my side, and our pinkies graze as he makes himself comfortable. His touch sends a different type of chill through me. And as we continue to chat, he doesn't move his pinky from mine.

"Me too. To answer your question, I've always envisioned myself making this home my permanent one. It's hard when I need to be in Tampa for the guys and, while it's only an hour's drive, I have always loved the convenience my condo provides." He looks at me contemplatively, his face faintly lit by the moonlight. I let my mind wander, envisioning Tate and myself hanging out on the beach every day with our growing blob. I think of Tate coming home and finding me swinging our blob on the back porch, and planting a gentle kiss on my forehead while I am taunted by the scent of grilling steaks. *What the fuck, D? Get that image out of your head right now, it's not happening.*

"Maybe one day you can find a way to make it work," I say, holding his gaze.

"Maybe." He says and with our proximity, I'm not sure if he's talking about living at the beach or us.

Chapter 8

Lasagna and Lilies

Tatum ‖ 15 weeks pregnant, September

In the weeks following our weekend at the beach house, the weight of our situation has been easier to carry. Every time I look at Darcy, I can't help but want more with her. I almost kissed her that night on the beach. She was wrapped in my sweatshirt, listening to me talk about my dream of living in that house. I can see that she wants it, too, but she's holding back. I've been waffling on asking her out on a proper date, but her job as a data analyst has been leaving her drained. So I am going to do the next best thing and text her best friend.

ME

What's her favorite meal?

KODI

Whose...?

ME

You know who.

KODI

Say it. Out loud.

Ugh, if she was anyone else I would be pissed but Kodi is just antagonizing me so that I have to face the facts. I want Darcy.

ME

Darcy. She's had a draining week, I want to have dinner ready so she doesn't have to worry about it.

KODI

You've never offered to cook meals for your friends before. Why are you really doing this?

ME

I told you why already and she's not just my friend.

KODI

What does that mean?

ME

I don't know yet. Now her favorite meal, please?

KODI

Lasagna, salad-hold the onions and garlic bread. The lady goes crazy for a homemade lasagna.

I chuckle, picturing Darcy jumping up and down when she discovers it's homemade. I also get a little hard imagining her letting one of her little moans loose like she did for the steaks.

ME

Thank you.

KODI

Don't hurt her, Tate. She doesn't let people in easily, and I can see her walls coming down with you. A kid adds another level of complication, so be careful.

ME

I don't intend to hurt her or our blob. I'm also not going to rush anything, if we progress past co-parenting, then we will take it one step at a time.

In between our texts, I order a delivery of everything I need to make Darcy dinner tonight.

KODI

Not you too with the Blob. LMFAO

ME

The baby looks like a blob right now so that's its nickname.

KODI

You two are odd. Bella is waking up, talk later. <3

I'm cleaning up the last bit of mess I made preparing dinner when I hear the front door click open softly. I wipe my sweaty hands down my pant legs, suddenly nervous that this small gesture is going to cross a boundary for her. Darcy's footsteps pad gently down the hallway, stopping in the kitchen doorway. Turning to her, she seems frozen in place, taking in the preset spots at the table, the fresh lilies in a vase in the center of the table, the lasagna dish, and a freshly tossed salad sitting next to a platter of garlic bread. For a little personal touch, I grabbed two Coke Icees right before I knew she would arrive, and they are sitting next to our plates, along with glasses of water.

"Dinner made for me twice in the past week? What did I do to deserve this?" She smiles softly before her eyes grow wide. "It smells delicious, lasagna?"

"Yep paired with a salad, no onions, and garlic bread," I explain, answering her smile with one of my own. I pull her seat out for her before taking my seat across from her.

"Who told you?" She questions, raising an eyebrow at me.

"Told me what exactly?"

"Lilies, lasagna, garlic bread. My three favorite things, I know for a fact I haven't told you that." She takes a bite of the lasagna and her eyes roll up into the back of her head. A perfect, gentle little moan escapes her lips as she swallows. My dick responds as it swells, reminding me how I'd like to see her swallow around something else.

"I wanted to do something for you. I know it's been rough at work recently. I texted Kodi, who helped point me in the right direction when it comes to your favorite food. Though, the lilies I picked out on my own. Lucky guess, I suppose." I pull at my neck anxiously, feeling my face flush.

"Well this lasagna is delicious, and the flowers are beautiful. Thank you, Tatum."

"Anytime. Can I ask you something?"

"Of course."

"Did you want kids? Like, before we found out about our blob."

She laughs, like wind chimes on a bright summer's day.

"I did. I don't think I wanted them right now, but I did eventually want one or two, maybe three. I didn't have siblings, or even cousins growing up. I was always envious of my friends who did."

"Having siblings is great until they're both girls and you can't get into the bathroom in the mornings. Honestly, I didn't ever plan on having kids." I pause for a deep breath, because I've never shared this next part with anyone before. "It's not because I didn't want to be a father, rather I didn't see how my lifestyle could adapt well enough for those kinds of changes. Like, beforehand I didn't think I would ever settle down with someone or want to sacrifice parts of my lifestyle—like getting a car that can hold a car seat."

"And now?" She asks, her voice timid.

"And now, I see that I was wrong. It'll be worth it, getting to hang out with our kid like Mav does with Bella. Seeing you blossom into the best mom and getting to co-parent with you feels right."

"You think I'm going to be the best mom?" Her pale skin taking on a pink hue.

"I do. Our little blob won the mom lottery." I smile. "Have you thought about how you want your career to fit in?"

She takes a moment before responding, carefully choosing how she wants to answer the question.

"Yes, and no. A conventional job, like the one I hold now, is something I would give up in a heartbeat. I barely have the energy to handle it now. No one knows this, except for the girls, but I've always wanted to write—and not some one-time passion project. I want to write something beautiful and powerful, like romance novels that make you scream, cry, kick your feet, and clench your thighs together." *Do not think about her thighs clenched together right now.* "I love how as an author I could make my schedule. I could write whenever I don't feel nauseous, during naps, or even during pumping sessions. It just takes time to see any kind of financial return out of it and I only have myself to rely on so I don't have the funds to do that right now."

"You know D-" I don't even get a chance to finish my thought before she gives me a "don't you dare" face.

"Absolutely not, Tatum."

"I didn't even get to tell you what I had in mind." I chide.

"You were going to offer to take over finances and say something too good to be true, like you have the money and I can focus on writing while you handle everything else. Were you not?"

"You got me there. But, Darcy, it's the truth. I make plenty enough to provide for us and I wouldn't mind helping you out while you build your brand and business. You would be able to rest when you need it, instead of working yourself into the ground. You can still be in charge of where our money goes." I pause, bracing myself for the potential backlash her fierce independence may cause. "Listen, Darcy, you don't have to say yes right now, or at all, even. Just think about it, okay?"

"Ugh, you have some valid points, but I don't want to say yes yet. The office is offering to let me work from home. They can see that I'm exhausted and want to work with me on some of that. I don't think they realize it's not the pregnancy sucking all my energy, it's the job. Do you mind if I set up an office space in my room to work?"

"You can do whatever you want, this condo is your home too, whether you say yes to my offer or not."

"Thank you, Tate."

"No problem, D."

A little while after cleaning up from dinner, we head to our respective rooms where I lay awake, wondering what life might look like over the coming months. Will Darcy's nausea ever completely go away? What kind of dad car will

I be driving or will we use hers to transport our blob? Will Darcy quit her job and take me up on my offer? When our child makes their appearance in the world, will anything change between Darcy and me? Will I be a good Dad? What does it feel like to hold your child for the first time?

Chapter 9

Extra Pickles Please

Tatum | 15 weeks pregnant, September

"**H**ey, how was the gym?" Darcy asks as I walk into the living room, her frizzy hair and droopy eyes implying she may have just woken up from a nap.

"Same old, same old. I'm going to grab a shower then we can tackle dinner?"

"That sounds great. I just took a quick nap, and haven't had lunch today." She grimaces, knowing I'm going to give her a hard time for not having eaten anything.

"Have you eaten at all today?"

"I had breakfast and some crackers here and there. Work was super busy, by the time I wrapped up all I wanted to do was sleep."

"Mama, you gotta eat. For you and the blob."

"I know. I need to be more intentional about eating." She sighs.

"Okay so whatcha want for dinner?"

"Hmmm, a burger and fries!"

"Sounds good to me. No onions right? Anything else?"

"Extra pickles please." After placing a delivery order, I head towards my room to grab my shower, while she disappears into her room.

"Knock, knock," I announce, entering her room twenty-five minutes later.

"Come in." She doesn't turn away, keeping focused on her computer.

"What are you doing over there?"

"Fleshing out the book plot I have in mind, just seeing if it's something I'm still inspired to write."

"Wanna tell me about it?" She slams her laptop shut with a definitive shake of her head. I take that as my cue to change the topic. "So you know the season is about to start up again right?"

"Yep, Kodi won't let me forget that Maverick will be leaving her *all* the time," she starts, with a roll of her eyes, "and I keep reminding her that I will have my child all by myself so she has it good."

"Hey, I will do whatever it takes to make it here when it's time. You can lean on me, you know that right?" I pack as much seriousness into my tone as I can, because there's no way I am missing the birth of our child.

"Um yeah, I guess I do now." She's twiddling her thumbs and won't look me in the eyes and of course, the bell rings to let our food delivery into the building.

"Be right back." I quickly gather the food, tipping the driver a little extra, and then head straight back to Darcy's room. We spread our food out on her bed before digging in, but she just picks at her burger, not eating, "Darcy what's going on? Is there something wrong with your food?"

"How often are you going to be gone?" She asks, catching me off guard. "What if there's an emergency?" She keeps her vision trained on her food, unwilling to look me in the eyes.

"Mama, look at me when I say these next words, and pay attention very carefully." Her gaze hesitantly lifts to meet mine. "While it's true that I'm going to be a lot busier managing the circus we call a professional hockey team during the season, and, yes, I will be going on some of their away game trips. However, I'm not needed at every single game, and if anything is to happen with you, I'm on the first flight out of whatever city I'm in to make it here to support you. If I can't get a flight, I'll get a car and I'll be here. Kind of like *Planes, Trains, and Automobiles*, but with the competence of a professional who handles the travel plans of NHL players." My emphasis is heavy on making it back to Darcy, showing her that I am putting her and our baby first, above all else. I feel like I'm in uncharted territory because I never imagined I would want to care for someone in this way. I'm helpless to control the curiosity I have for the little changes in our baby day after day, and watching Darcy's stomach grow with our child—which has only sped up over the last couple of weeks.

"I'm scared, Tate," Darcy confesses with a sniffle, her beautiful browns brimming with liquid emotion. A single tear escapes down her cheek and I instinctively reach out, softly swiping it away with my thumb.

"I am too, D. We may feel a little in over our heads here but I know that as long as we have each other's backs, we'll be okay. So will the little one."

I lean back against her headboard with open arms, beckoning her to my side. Making her way around the bed, Darcy positions herself beside me, resting her head on my shoulder. Her body shakes as her emotional dam lets loose, her tears threatening to drown the whole world. I hold her to me, wanting nothing but to be the safe space she needs to let her emotions out. Eventually, her breathing evens out, and she finishes with a final, cathartic, heavy breath.

"I should probably eat now. You're right about us having each other's backs, but every day I feel like a new fear pops up and it can overwhelm me. Like, I was thinking today, what if I sneeze too hard and rupture my amniotic sac, causing me to go into preterm labor? So of course I called Sin in tears. She said that if I leak when I sneeze, it's probably just pee." She shrugs, laughing at herself, and moves to grab her burger before leaning back into my arms. I don't typically do nonsexual intimacy, but with Darcy, moments like these make me question why I never cared to—something about her defies everyone who came before, and I realize that I want this. I want her.

"It's healthy to be scared by all these changes. We don't have the slightest clue what to expect throughout the next six months. Except that, in the end, we get a sweet little blob to bring home and love on for the rest of our lives." I chuckle.

"Thanks, Tate. I feel better after airing out some of my fears." She yawns. "I think I'm going to shower and hit the hay."

"I think that's a good idea. Don't be afraid to talk to me, Darcy. Please." I meander to my room, flopping back onto my bed with the fresh realization that I'm in deeper with her than I thought. I text Maverick, needing someone to help me unpack the conflict swirling in my head.

ME

Dude. I think I have feelings for Darcy.

MAVERICK

No duh dipshit. Nice of you to finally
admit it.

ME

Not helpful man.

MAVERICK

It doesn't have to be this hard dude, ask
her out.

ME

This coming from the man who fought his
feelings for his wife for months before she
had to force his hand.

MAVERICK

And look at me now, a whole ass husband.

What's stopping you?

ME

I'm scared I'll hurt her, man. I don't do
romantic relationships, I haven't in a really
long time.

MAVERICK

She could be the one to change that. Do
you really want to pass that up?

ME

BUT if I hurt her... I lose them both.

My fears and doubts crash into me again, relentlessly.

MAVERICK

Kodi says, "Don't forget that I will castrate
you if you hurt them." But she also says to
let it happen naturally because if it's meant
to be, it will work out okay.

Katelyn Snyder

ME

> YOU TOLD HER AGAIN MAN?
> SERIOUSLY?!?

MAVERICK

> Husband/wife privilege. What do you expect when you text me at night—the woman literally sleeps on my chest. She's privy to anything that might be on my phone. Good luck… Speaking of my wife, I have to go take care of something.

ME

> TMI dude. Goodnight.

Chapter 10

Game Night

Tatum ‖ 16 weeks pregnant, October

"Is it weird to you that your family wants me to attend these things, even though we aren't together?" Darcy sits in the passenger seat of the Porsche worrying her bottom lip.

"Nope," I refute, popping the P for emphasis as we approach my family home for our first official Reed family game night.

"Ah, there they are!" Mom squeals, as we approach the front porch where she sits, sipping on her Chamomile tea as she has done almost every evening since I can remember.

"Rose!" Darcy graces my mom with a blinding, genuine smile, pulling her in for a hug.

"How have you been feeling sweetie?" My mom asks Darcy, still holding her close.

"Better, more tired than anything," Darcy replies.

"Hi, Mom. I'm still here, your son, that you birthed," I say, butting in.

"Oh, you hush up now. I've had almost thirty years of

hugging you, and my Darcy hugs have some catching up to do. Now get over here," teases my mom, as she releases Darcy and pulls me into her arms.

"Let's get inside. Your sisters are dying to see you both." Sure enough, Tessa and Tinsley are waiting eagerly for us just inside.

"OMG! Look at your little bump," Tessa squeals, softly reaching out to Darcy's stomach with the same awe that I did, despite it being only slightly bigger than it was when we came to tell them she was pregnant.

"Ugh, you are so cute!" Tinsley sings, before also reaching out.

"Girls, maybe let's show some respect and ask Darcy before we just touch her body." My mom scolds them and they immediately retract their hands with reddened cheeks.

"Oh, no! It's okay! Go ahead girls, although there's not much to feel yet." Darcy steps closer to the twins and they eagerly reach out again.

Dad steps in from the living room, "Ribs are just about ready."

Darcy looks at me with suspicious eyes and I just shrug. Allegedly, I told Dad that Darcy had mentioned that she would do some naughty things for a rack of ribs—leaving out the part about doing naughty things. I didn't push further to know what things she would do at the time. I did, however, come in my bed that night, envisioning her doing some very filthy things with me. Without my permission, my cock begins to swell. But now is not the time to relive those thoughts—my family is standing two feet away from us. *Grandmas, dead puppies, pimple-popping videos.* Yep, that did the trick.

"The blob and I are starving," Darcy says with a smirk,

before my dad gently pushes my sisters to the side and pulls her into a hug.

"Let's eat, then." Mom claps her hands and we all disperse to our seats in the dining room.

"Do you know if you're giving us a niece or nephew yet?" Tinsley asks as we pass around the plate of ribs that smell divine. Sweet but savory scents swirl around us.

"We will find out in a few weeks." Darcy imparts, beaming at my sister, and moves quickly to scoop potato salad onto hers and my plates.

"Thank you," I say, passing the bowl over to my dad.

"Seems late? I went at sixteen weeks with the girls and Tate." My mom asks.

"Tate is out of town for work that week, so we scheduled it during the nineteenth week," Darcy replies.

"Will you do a gender reveal?" Asks Mom. Surprisingly, we haven't talked about it, so I turn to Darcy, curious to see what she thinks.

"Um, we haven't decided yet, but I know my friends will make a huge deal out of planning a baby shower. Maybe for a gender reveal," offers Darcy, gesturing at her and me, "we can do something just for us. What do you think, Tate?"

"I think that sounds great." Before my sisters have a chance to complain, I add, "Don't worry we will still make sure everyone finds out in a video or something."

"Oh good, no way do I want to miss your reaction," Tessa says in my direction, "I think you're going to cry."

I roll my eyes, "Maybe I will, maybe I won't."

"Son, I said the same thing, and I cried like a baby when we found out we were having a boy. Then, I cried even harder when we found out we were having two girls... at the same time." My dad jokes and we all laugh together.

"Who wants pie?" Mom asks, already headed into the kitchen.

"Rose dear, let's wait a little while on the pie. Maybe play a round of Scrabble while our stomachs settle." Dad hollers in the direction of the kitchen.

"I'm stuffed," I groan, leaning back into my chair.

"Me too, but the blob will want some pie in like an hour or two," Darcy adds.

"Me three." My sisters say in unison. I swear they share the same brain or can read each other's minds or something. This happens all the time.

"Fine. Let me beat your butts in Scrabble then," declares Mom.

"Coagulated. Fourteen points, triple word score. Forty-two points. Read it and weep, bitches!" Darcy yells, immediately covering her mouth, flush with embarrassment. "Oh my god, I am so sorry."

"And here I thought *I* was competitive," I laugh, slightly aroused by her now-untethered competitive spirit.

"Looks like that's a game." Mom looks frustrated about losing to Darcy by the slimmest of margins. "I'm going to go heat the pie." My dad follows closely behind her, likely to ensure she doesn't carry over her frustration into the next game.

"Is she mad?" Darcy asks, furtively looking towards my sisters and me.

"Definitely. Mom is a bit competitive." Tess says.

"That's why Tatum was so good at hockey when he

played. He got dad's build and mom's combined competitive spirit." Tinsley adds and my jaw immediately tightens at the revelation I used to play. I can't be mad at my sisters, they don't know Darcy is unaware of that part of my past.

"Wait... you played?" Darcy's eyes are the size of dinner plates.

"Yes, but we can talk about it on the way home. I don't want to talk about it right now," I stress, a little too defensively, Darcy's eyes immediately welling with tears. I didn't intend to be so harsh, and I regret my tone as soon as the words have left my mouth.

"Excuse me." Darcy stands, swiftly exiting the room before I can even apologize.

"Cover for us," I plead quietly, pointing at the twins. I turn, following in Darcy's footsteps before they can even respond. I find the bathroom door is slightly ajar and the lights are on. Not even bothering to knock, I push into the cramped space to find Darcy sitting on the side of the tub wiping tears away from her eyes.

"Mama." She doesn't look at me so I squat down in front of her, cupping her chin with my hand and forcing her to look at me. "Mama," I repeat, this time the focus of her attention, "I'm sorry for being rude back there. I want to tell you. My personal history with the game is a touchy subject and I don't want to rehash it in my family's living room. "

Her eyes bore into mine for a moment, before she grabs my wrist where it's captivating her gaze. "You can't talk to me like that, jerkface."

"I'm sorry, D. You're right, and I promise to tell you about it on the drive home, okay?"

"Fine." That's all she says before letting go of my hand, standing, and attempting to walk around me.

"Nope, come here." I'm up before she has time to react,

pulling her into my arms, "I'm not letting go until you return the hug."

"You're so annoying and I'm still mad at you." Still, she wraps her arms around me, returning my hug, and I breathe in her vanilla scent.

"That's on me. Let's go see how many more times we can beat my mom at board games." This causes a small, poorly stifled laugh to escape her and I let her go, following her into the living room.

"You guys okay?" Dad asks as we enter the room, six slices of untouched pie sitting around a Monopoly board.

"All good." Darcy gives him a stiff smile and takes a seat, lifting her piece of pie into her mouth.

"DRIVE SAFE, text us when you get home, please. Love you both!" Mom shouts, from her position on the porch, wrapped in my dad's arms. Shutting Darcy's door behind her, I head to the driver's side.

"You got it! Love you both," I call back, and slide in to see Darcy blowing them a kiss from her seat. The way she feels comfortable with my family gives me a warmth that radiates from deep within my chest. I hope she feels the love my parents have for her.

"Alright, Reed, get talking." She says before I've even made it out of the driveway.

"Getting right into it then, love," I tut, in another of my infamous horrible accents attempting to disarm my discomfort, "No tea or casual conversation in the parlor first?"

"Not right now, Tate. I need to know what got you so

bent out of shape earlier." She doesn't play along with me, which can only mean Darcy is serious about us having this conversation while tonight's events are still fresh in our memory.

"When I was in high school," I begin, pausing briefly to clear my throat, "I wanted to play a sport. Basketball never appealed to me, I've never been a particularly good swimmer, baseball felt too slow, and football felt too aggressive."

"And hockey didn't?" She interrupts me, a shocked laugh leaving her mouth.

"You'd think. Hockey appealed to me because it felt the most competitive, and once I got out on the ice, I was a natural—moving like a rocket according to my coach and my mom. They named me right winger my sophomore year, and by my senior year, I was captain. Wingers tend to only be aggressive if necessary—or if they are Dominic Montez." I glimpse her smile out of my periphery before I pick up where I left off. "I was offered a full-ride athletic scholarship to Florida U with the condition that I played for the team. My parents and I briefly discussed it before I gladly accepted the offer. The first two years went great, I led the team, aced my classes, and even met a girl." I leave out that, the only relationship I've ever been in, led to me never wanting to commit to another person, sacrificing the life I enjoy for one person.

"You met a girl?" She sounds confused, like the possibility of me dating anyone was otherworldly.

I don't blame her. I have a reputation for being single and enjoying a comfortable bachelor lifestyle. For a long time, I just enjoyed my time with women, and then we'd mutually agree to head in separate directions. I've always set a clear boundary with them.

"We'll get to that in a moment. Picture this, it's senior

year and I'm being scouted by multiple NHL teams. I've got the girl that I might spend the rest of my life with and we are in the final college championship game. I'm speeding down the ice with the puck towards Missouri's net when I get checked into the board at full force." I pause for a moment, talking about this takes me right back to that moment. The screams from the fans, the way my body buckled underneath me, the blinding pain I felt as it happened. "My right kneecap goes straight into the board with the most horrific cracking sound and I'm on the ground immediately. I got rushed to the ER to find out that the way my leg twisted after the check twisted quite a few ligaments in my leg including my ACL."

"Oh my god, that's awful."

"We did a surgery to stabilize my knee cap and an ACL reconstruction surgery. I did physical therapy for six months but was never able to reach my full form back. I missed my chance to be drafted. To top it off, the girl only stuck with me in hopes that I would recover and she would become a WAG, maybe even Mrs. Reed. When I told her I was no longer going to be playing, she broke up with me."

"I'm so sorry you went through that, Tatum." Darcy sniffles from her seat beside me, tears falling down her face. I gently place my hand on her thigh, squeezing lightly.

"Don't cry for me, Mama, I'm happy now." She places her hand over mine on her leg, not removing my hand or squeezing but just letting it rest there.

"Does it still bother you?"

"Once in a while I get a little stiff, but it's manageable. It's part of why I put so much effort into staying in shape."

"Is this why you wanted to work in the NHL? To stay close to the game?"

"It is. I graduated with a business degree, and it worked

out where I was able to get my foot in the door with the Mantas." We pull into the gated underground garage for our condo building as I answer her.

"Do you miss playing?" Darcy asks in a solemn tone.

"Yeah, I do, but I'm happy where I ended up. Had I kept playing, I may not have stayed in Tampa, or I could have reinjured myself and made it worse. I might not have met Mav, who met Kodi, who then brought you into my life." With that, I park the car and we head to the elevator that will take us up to our condo.

"I suppose I'm glad, then, that it didn't work out the way you hoped." Darcy smiles at me from across the elevator, her hand rubbing circles on her small bump. The sight sends butterflies rampant in my stomach.

Chapter 11

No Questions, Comments, Concerns

Darcy ‖ 16 weeks pregnant, October

The smell of chlorine swirls with burning charcoal as we walk into Kodi and Maverick's backyard, carrying the cupcakes we were asked to pick up. It's Stu, Mav's father, sixtieth birthday today so everyone is here to celebrate. While I want to spend time with my friends and pseudo-parents, I'm feeling grumpy. I hate the way my black one-piece is sitting on my body. Tatum, on the other hand, is wearing a tank top that shows off his tattooed bicep and a pair of slutty little swim shorts—their five-inch inseam doesn't leave much to the imagination.

Tatum stops me short of rounding the corner of the home before anyone sees us. "You alright?"

"Yes." Clearly tuned into the fact that I'm not alright, he says nothing in response but raises a golden eyebrow. "Fine. I just feel cranky today. My mom has called like three times today, and I don't like the way this bathing suit feels."

His eyes roam over my body. I've got shorts on and an oversized shirt in my bag for later. Although I'm mostly covered, the way he's taking me in has my heart doing cannonballs inside my rib cage.

"I think your bump is adorable. You don't owe your mom anything but you should call her back if you're worried."

"Ugh, I don't know if I want to."

"As far as the grumpiness, anything I can do?"

"Get me a snack, and *don't* let Dom splash me. And, thank you."

"Done and done. Let's do this." In a move I wasn't expecting he grabs my hand and leads me around the corner. I can't tell if everyone's eyes actually turn towards us only to get stuck on our interlocked hands, or if maybe it just feels that way. I immediately remove mine from his, smiling sheepishly. A dismayed look passes over Tatum's face, barely noticeable as he turns to grab the snacks he promised me.

Kodi, Sin, and Harley sit on the pool ledge, drinks in hand and feet in the water watching Collins, Dom, and Bella swim back and forth together. Bella's bright pink floaties and Collins' watchful eye keeping her above water. Maverick and Nik, as always man the grill while Victoria, Dale, and Jason sit around a large plastic table set up under a white canopy tent. Grace exits the house with Stu, heading towards the pool.

"Happy birthday!" I holler at Stu, Mav's father, as he steps down the patio, he makes his way towards me pulling me into his arms.

"Darcy, do you remember my daughter Grace and her husband, Jason, from the wedding?" Asks Stu.

"Yes, hi. Good to see you again." They give me cordial smiles before returning to their trek to the pool. I head over to the picnic table, my last stop before I plop down beside my girls on the pool ledge.

"Hi, Momma." I beam at Victoria, Kodi's mom, who treats me as her adopted daughter. When we were younger she always gave me a safe space to get away from my overbearing parents. Victoria always felt like the kind of parent I longed for, someone who listened and understood my dreams—just as she does for Kodi.

"Oh, sweet girl. Look at you!" She's up and around the table before I've made it three steps. Her gentle hands grasping my shoulders, she coos, "Are you feeling better? Kodi said you were having a hard time the first few weeks."

"Much, thank you for asking." I lean in, "Introduce me to your new man." She blushes but guides me over to Dale who stands with an outstretched hand.

"Mom, can we have our bestie now?" Kodi turns over her shoulder, teasing her Mom.

"I suppose you can. I was just catching up with my other daughter." Victoria rolls her eyes but shoos me away, taking her seat back by Dale, her return welcomed with a possessive arm around her.

"Hi, my loves." I wiggle my fingers towards my friends as I take a seat, leaning my head into Sin beside me.

I'm hardly sitting for a moment before a water bottle and plate full of veggies, fruits, what looks to be a ranch, and a caramel dip appear in front of my face. "Your snack madam. Dominic has been warned about splashing purposefully."

"Thank you." I turn my head up to Tatum, smiling at him. A gleam of sweat on his brow, black sunglasses covering his eyes, a smirk firmly planted on his face.

Sin watches Tate walk away before whisper-shouting,

"Holy fuck that man is hot. I see why you let him knock you up."

"I didn't let him. It was an accident." I gently jab her in the stomach with my elbow. "He is hot though, isn't he?" This causes all of us to giggle.

"I have to head out soon." Harley sighs dejectedly. I don't know what has gotten under her skin, but she seems to be withdrawn. She shows up, but lately she isn't actively in conversation and she always leaves early.

"What? Why?" Kodi whines. I munch on a carrot stick watching this conversation take place.

"I have to study, then meet up with Benji."

"He could've joined us, you know." I can see Sin's eye roll from out of the corner of mine.

"Yeah, well, he isn't here, is he? He had plans, but still wanted to see me at some point." Harley snaps. Down wind of Harley's slightly raised tone, Collins' head whips around from where he floats on the other end of the pool. Why would she waste time with butthead Benji, when Collins is so very clearly ready to give her his full attention? I will never understand.

"Jesus, Harls, sorry." Sin sounds defeated, making me question how many times she's had to deal with this temper.

"You know what? I think I'm going to head out now." Harley stands abruptly and—just as fast—Collins is out of the pool telling Dom to watch Bella and following her out of the yard just as fast. Their muffled shouts can be heard, not enough to make out any words, but their tone couldn't be more clear.

"Well, that sucked." Kodi rubs her temples, "I hope Harls is okay."

"Yeah, same here," I sigh, truly worried about a member

of my tight knit inner-circle. Collins returns ten minutes later but joins the guys at the grill.

"Want to hear some hot team gossip?" Kodi almost-whispers, as if she is afraid someone will hear her telling us news we aren't supposed to know yet.

"Yes!" We all squeal in her direction.

"Conrad Hoyer got traded to the Manta Rays," she discloses, seemingly unphased by the news.

"No way! How is Maverick feeling about that?" I gasp. Why is she so cool with it?

"How are *you* feeling about it?" Sin chimes in.

"I mean, Mav doesn't care. I'm his wife, after all. He's a team player, so he's not going to do anything less than try to make him feel welcome. I guess Conrad's attitude is making it all a little difficult, though. And, I don't care, as long as he doesn't act like a douchecanoe again, I'll play nice." She smiles sweetly but I know beneath that smile she's not joking—she will play nice until she's given a reason not to.

I hum in response, thinking about what our little group would look like if Conrad became part of it and then shaking it off because that doesn't sound ideal.

"Food's ready!" Nik hollers. Sinclair helps me stand, worried that I can't lift myself off the ground and presuming it's better I have her assistance—much to my ire.

Chatter, water splashing, and singing Happy Birthday are the soundtrack of the rest of the afternoon. By the time Tatum and I return to the condo, my body feels heavy, my head hurts, and I know that I need to rest. Tatum can tell, too, asking if he can get me anything. I turn him down, taking my giant water jug to my bed with me.

I thought I had finally seen the other side of my pregnancy nausea era, but I was wrong. This past week has been miserable, I'm peeling myself out of bed just to sit at my desk and toil away in a monotonous job. I run to the bathroom almost every time I eat and find small tasks like doing my dishes or laundry to be over-exhausting. If I'm not working, I'm laying in my bed or on the couch doing nothing. I find myself thinking back to Tatum's offer to pay my bills while I focus on nurturing the blob and writing my debut novel. Something is holding me back, my fear of relying on someone else and losing my independence again just like with my parents, maybe?

Deciding that asking for Harley's opinion could be good practice for *her*, I call my friend.

"Hey, D, what's up?" A door slams in the background causing me to flinch.

"What was that, Harls?" Concern is at the forefront of my mind because I know Sin wouldn't be slamming doors in the apartment they share. Between her weird behavior at Stu's birthday, and now this, I'm growing more concerned.

"Oh nothing, just Benji leaving for work." Harley is always quiet but usually when she speaks, there's some inflection in her voice. Right now, there is none.

She's lying.

"You know you can talk to me, right?" I pry, aware that I can't push too hard or she'll shut me out.

"Yeah Darcy, everything is fine. We are fine. Leave it alone. Did you need something?" She is rarely this short with anyone.

"I need you to therapize me." Reading her hostility, loud and clear, I change topics to keep her talking to me. If I had the energy, I would be pacing back and forth in my room right now.

"Okay, well, tell me what's going on." She laughs, but it's strained.

"Hey, you aren't supposed to laugh at your clients."

"You aren't my client, you are my friend taking advantage of my education in this field."

"Fine. You can't see me but I just rolled my eyes at you. A few weeks back, Tatum was about to offer me money for my bills so that I could focus on writing and resting. Well, I cut him off. I will *not* rely on him for that. It feels too much like I'm back in my parents' grasp, someone else having control over my money and my life."

"But you said he was going to give you the money, right, not pay the bills directly?"

"Yeah..." I already know where she is going with this and I am starting to regret my decision to call her.

"So who has control of the money if he's giving it directly to you?"

"Ugh, me..."

"Right. So, what *else* is holding you back?" She prods, and I take a moment to think about it.

"I think... relying on him makes this feel more like a relationship...but it's not one. However, I can't help myself from wanting it to be one..."

"Why does relying on him make it feel like a relationship?"

"Because you just don't rely on a platonic friend to give you money and let you stay home and chase your dreams while caring for the child you created together," I huff.

"It sounds like someone is offering to do something nice

for you, and you are too scared to admit your feelings for him." Harley sees right through me, and I hate it.

"God dammit Harley. You're going to be a great fucking therapist soon."

"I know." I can almost see her cheeky little grin through the phone.

We stay on the phone for another thirty minutes talking in circles, until Harley gives up and chirps, "If this is what you want D, then just go for it."

"Okay, I'll talk to him. Love you, Harls. Call if you need to talk."

"I will, D. Love you too." The call ends and I gear myself up to accept Tatum's very gracious offer, but not before texting Sin and Ko about what just happened with Harley.

ME

I'm worried about Harls. She just snapped at me over the phone.

SIN

She hasn't been home for more than a day or two in weeks.

KODI

It's Benji, it has to be.

ME

What do we do?

SIN

Keep an eye on her, prepare the pitchforks, and show up at his apartment if she stops responding altogether. She's at least talking to us still. I don't know but I want my Harls back.

KODI

Me too.

ME

Me three.

I'm sitting on the condo balcony reading a very spicy monster romance, when the glass door slides open behind me. I quickly lock my Kindle, because how the heck would I tell the father of my child that dragons dominating human women gets my rocks off? Hell no. Not right now at least.

"Welcome home." I try to school my expression. Tatum just happened to walk in on a very intense scene that is soon to be included in my 'book scenes that live rent-free in my head' note on my phone. "How was work?"

"Dominic was supposed to do an ad with the local shelter, but he's refusing to step into the shelter because, and I quote, 'I cannot end up with a dog in my house. This is a recipe for me to end up with one.' So, then Collins stepped in, and he got suckered into bringing home a mouthy white kitten, with the brightest green eyes. He named her Precious. Somehow it's my fault when we were just doing a partnership where if people brought in their adoption certificate then they would get a free drink at the arena to help clear the shelter," he explains, taking a seat on the black loveseat beside me.

"Oh, and I called around and found a place that we can drop the gender results off to and they can have a cake ready in twenty-four hours." He tacks on.

"Yay, I'm so excited. Sounds like quite the day." I chuckle, "Dom would have left with like three dogs if he did that ad. Didn't think Collins was a cat guy, but it makes sense."

"Yeah, I guess he's always wanted one, and this was just an excuse for him to take the leap. How was your day?"

"Honestly... exhausting, and would you believe I had a really weird conversation with Harley? But, that's neither here nor there."

We sit in peaceful silence watching the city pass us by for a bit. I twiddle my thumbs staring out over the river, cars beeping, people giggling as they walk by the water, the bright lights casting a warm glow on the dim streets below. I spend the time readying myself to spit out my appreciation for Tate's offer and that I'd like to take him up on it.

I have this horrible trait of just ripping the bandaid off when it comes to Tatum, rather than attempting to sugar-coat a conversation with him. Eventually, the anxiety spills out, and I blurt, "*I have decided to graciously accept the good sir's offer of patronage.*" Pulling out the debutante's voice is just the icing on top of the cake.

"*Tally-ho, fair maiden, we must begin making arrange-ments immediately,*" Tatum chokes out, struggling to contain his infectious laugh. He clears his throat before adding, "Are you serious?"

"Um..." I start, clearing my throat in return, "Yes, I would like to use the time to work on my debut novel and to prepare for and nurture the baby."

"Okay."

"That's all? No other questions, comments, concerns..."

"Nope. I left the offer on the table and I still want to help. We agreed the money will go to you, for you to do with what you will.. Once it's in your hands, it's out of mine and I don't need—or want—to know where it's going. It's none of my business."

I struggle to wrap my head around what his reason for doing this is. "Sorry, it's just... With my Dad, money was a big way he tried to hold control over my life. So I think I prepared myself to give you every single detail." I exhale a deep breath, reining my thoughts in. "Thank you, Tate. It means so much that you are willing to do this."

He smiles softly at me now, his right dimple more prominent than his left. His hazel green eyes sparkling in the dim city lights. I find myself drawing into him, scooting closer and wrapping my arms around him. My head rests gently against his shoulder as he wraps his dress shirt-clad arm around me.

"I'll do anything for you, Darcy."

It's barely a murmur, but I heard it loud and clear. Not only does my heart react to his quiet pledge, its beat hastening, but for some unholy reason my pussy decides it's the perfect time to start its own palpitations. I need to get the heck out of here before I do something stupid—like pounce on him right here on this far too public balcony.

"You don't mean that." I try to laugh it off, but he isn't laughing with me, killing mine as quickly as it bubbled out of me. Deciding there has never been a better time for a quick escape, I pull myself from his grasp and stand awkwardly. Unable to contain myself, I circle back to my debutante accent. "*Good heavens I think 'tis past my bedtime.* Thanks again, Tate."

"Goodnight, Mama." Clearly able to tell that I'm beyond flustered he winks at me, and I hightail it to the privacy of my bedroom.

After a very quick and very cold shower that I desperately hoped would take the edge off, I lie in bed for what feels like hours. I can't get comfortable, moving restlessly from side to side. Staring wide-eyed at my ceiling, failing to escape into my monster romance, attempting to orchestrate my debut—my brain refuses to cooperate and all I can think about is *Tatum fucking Reed*. His piercing eyes, the way he calls me Mama, the feeling of his veiny, circumcised cock sliding in and out of me. It's all escalated so quickly and now my nipples are hard and I'm rubbing my thighs together eager to ease some of the tension.

Fuck it. No one is going to know unless I tell them. How could they know? I reach into my nightstand, pulling out a small, black clit stimulator before doing away with my shorts and spreading my legs. I drift my fingers along my body, pausing to pinch and pull at my tender nipples, before introducing them to my arousal.

"Jesus Christ, what is this man *doing* to me?" I whisper breathlessly to absolutely no one. I turn the vibrator on its middle setting, my carefully perfected amount of stimulation. With a soft and steady touch, I center my favorite toy onto my bundle of nerves, hissing at the feeling briefly before settling into it. I let my eyes drift close and replay the night of Kodi and Maverick's wedding. I'm trying to be quiet but helpless to stop the small whimpers and moans that escape my lips as I make myself cum to my fantasy of more pleasure-filled nights with Tatum.

Chapter 12

Metaphorical Knees

Tatum ‖ 17 weeks pregnant, October

I didn't mean to say out loud that I'd do anything for her. It just slipped out, spurred by the weight of her arms around me and her faint vanilla scent wafting into my nose. I mean it, though. Watching her bear our child has me feeling a fierce sense of protectiveness over her heart, her mind, fuck even her body.

Darcy went to lie down after our conversation, and as I'm passing by her bedroom door I overhear faint whimpers emanating from within. At first, I think that she's crying, or maybe not feeling well. But, as I edge closer to the door—tempted to stick my ear against it like some peeping Tom—her whimpers turn into pleasure-filled moans and I find myself stopped dead in my tracks.

My cock immediately grows stiff in my slacks. The faint buzz of a vibrator softly carries outside the room and I think back about our first, and only, night together. I relive the way that her pussy stretched around my fingers as I pumped them into her, the way her back arched in the throes of her orgasm, and I wonder if she ever masturbates while she thinks about us. My hands move of their own accord, and I unbutton my pants, pulling my cock out, and slowly stroke it in the middle of the hallway. *Jesus, I am acting like a horny teenager.*

As her moans become louder and more erratic, I pump my cock faster, my forehead falling lightly against the door. I bite my lip to stifle a groan when she lets out one last, long sigh of pleasure, and I imagine her body writhing beneath mine as she comes. Following her over the edge, I cum all over my hand. Careful not to make a mess, I stuff myself back into my underwear and head to my bedroom to clean myself before falling into bed for a fitful night's sleep.

Darcy has one last week of her job before she can focus on writing and resting. At that point, her rest and hydration are going to be the priority. Her nausea came back with a vengeance last week. She says she isn't vomiting as much as she was, but she's miserable and on the verge of upchucking every time she eats.

I've fallen into a routine of finding her curled up on the couch, a giant jug of water in hand, and Gilmore Girls playing on repeat in the background. She loves it so much that I've covertly been watching it in my room at night, trying to catch up to her current season. Today though, I came home to pervasive silence, and she's not on the couch where she typically lays.

"D?" I holler into the condo, to no response. I check the kitchen and balcony, to no avail, before heading towards her bedroom. Her door is cracked, but the room is dark and full of the same silence that's greeted me elsewhere in our home. I knock, and gently call out, "Darcy?" Still, nothing, so I push in and see her small form curled up in the middle of the bed under her favorite, purple and fuzzy blanket.

"Hi." She's quiet, sounding dispirited.

"What's going on Mama?" I ask, approaching the bed and sitting on the edge beside her, placing a hand gently on her forehead to make sure she's not running a fever.

"I'm just really tired and the vomiting gave me a migraine," she mewls.

"Can I do anything? Have you eaten?" Side-eyeing the very full water jug on her nightstand, I know she's possibly dehydrated—especially if she's unable to keep her water down.

"I just woke up. I had some eggs and toast this morning, but then I fell asleep. " Fuck. It's been almost nine hours. It's hard when eating makes her nauseous, but I don't want her passing out when I'm not around. I'm going to have to get the girls over here while I'm at work.

"Can I get you something? Maybe some chicken soup? Or rice? A banana?"

"Mmm, soup sounds good."

"Be right back." I gently squeeze her leg. "Try to drink some water, please." I'm down the hallway and pulling a can of soup from the pantry in a dash. I pull out my phone while heating the soup on the stovetop. I call Harley first— her school schedule offers her the most free time, but her voicemail greets me. I try Sinclair next, saving Kodi for last. It might be hard for Kodi to manage both Arabella and Darcy.

"Tatum, to what do I owe the pleasure?" Sin's silky, smooth voice comes through the phone.

"I need to call in a favor. Darcy's nausea came roaring back, she's been prone to migraines. When I got home from work today, she hadn't eaten since this morning. Please tell me you're off the next few days and can come sit with her while I'm gone?" Metaphorically or not, I am not above getting on my knees and begging Sin to help me with Darcy.

"You're lucky she's one of my best friends. I was supposed to spend the next few days resting and hopefully getting some action," She jeers, her tone laced with aggravation.

"Well, I tried Harley, but she didn't answer. I think it would be too hard for Kodi with Bella running around. Plus you're the nurse, so she'll have to listen to you. I will pay for you to get a massage every month for the next year, Sin, please." I stir the soup in the pot, noticing it's beginning to boil. I turn to grab a bowl with my phone tucked in between my ear and shoulder. I pour it into the bowl before carefully making my way towards Darcy's room. "I'm bringing her soup as we speak."

"Whoa, you care about her don't you?" Sin, of all people, is the one to call me out but, at this point, it no longer matters. I do care about Darcy and I do intend to make her mine if or when she's willing to give herself to me.

"I do."

"What time do you head in tomorrow? Try to focus on getting her fed and bathed tonight then just let her rest."

"Around ten in the morning, it's a pretty light day."

"Perfect, see you then."

"Thanks again, Sin." With that, she hangs up and I push Darcy's door open. She's sitting up now, head resting against the headboard, her eyes half open, with purple bags making them appear sunken in.

"Here ya go, D. Try and eat some. I'm going to start you a bath." She takes the bowl from me and begins slowly but surely eating it as I enter her bathroom. I haven't been in here since she moved in. Inside, her vanilla scent is overpowering, an array of beauty products lies skewed across the counter, and a bright pink hairbrush sits on the counter with blonde hairs intertwined between the bristles. She's added a fluffy rug in front of the counter and another aqua one sits in front of the shower. The shower curtain is patterned in tiny disco balls and ghosts wearing cowboy hats. I move it to the side and turn the faucet on, testing its warmth before plugging the drain. Peeking under her cabinet, I find Epsom salts that I throw in along with some of the bubble liquid she has sitting on the edge of the tub. I don't want the bright bathroom light on for her, so I grab a candle and lighter sitting on the back of her toilet, letting its soft flame illuminate the bathroom.

"Your bath is ready." I exit the bathroom and see the soup bowl is empty, sitting on the bedside table, but she has laid back down—the cool rag I brought in earlier draped over her eyes as she gently rubs circles over her temples.

"I can't." She sniffles.

I can't believe I'm about to offer this especially after my cock was in my hand about twenty feet away from here last night so seeing her naked is probably the last thing I need to do right now.

"Would you be okay if I lifted you?"

"You don't have to do that. I can just shower when I'm feeling better."

"I know, but I want to. I think it may help, especially now that you've eaten."

"Ugh, fine." She reluctantly lifts herself to a sitting position, swaying a little. "I'm too light-headed to argue."

I step towards her, placing one arm around her back and the other under her legs, and carry her into the bathroom. I stand her on her feet, helping her stay steady as she pulls her shirt over her head. I keep my eyes firmly focused on the little freckle she has above her left eyebrow.

"I need you to take my pants off, Tatum, because I don't think leaning over right now is the right move."

I'd love to hear her ask me to take off her pants in any other circumstance, but here my sole focus is making sure she's cared for and hopefully feeling a bit better afterwards. I grasp the waistband of her sweats, pushing them down and holding her steady as she steps out of them and into the tub.

I take a seat on the edge of the tub. We sit in silence for a moment before I lean over and get two pumps of her shampoo and gently rub it into her scalp. She relaxes into my touch, her eyes drifting closed. I probably spend more time than necessary to lather her hair, getting a little carried away.

"Do you want to brush your hair with some conditioner, or after you're out?"

"Probably with the conditioner." Her eyes remain closed and she seems to be the most relaxed she's been since I got home. I can't help but feel a little pride over helping her to feel this way. After rinsing her hair out and then letting the conditioner sit, I run her hairbrush gently through her head, working the knots out and avoiding jostling her head around too much.

"You ready to get your body washed and then I'll help you get to bed?"

"You are being such a mama bird right now." She sighs at me, sounding exasperated. Her attitude coming back is a good sign. She pulls the drain before slowly standing and turning the showerhead on before shooing me and pulling the curtain closed. I relocate to the closed toilet seat.

"Maybe I am, but coming home and finding you sheltering in the dark while not having eaten all day warrants a little overzealous care for you." I contemplate telling her that Sin will be here tomorrow before just spitting it out. "And Sin is coming to sit with you tomorrow."

"I don't need a babysitter, Tate." She sticks her hand out of the shower with a 'give me' motion and I grab and place her fluffy pink towel in her hand.

"I feel compelled to make sure you're okay since I have some long days coming up. Just think of it like some bestie time."

"It's Sin. She's going to be all over me." I know and it's exactly why I want her here, but Darcy doesn't need to know that. The shower curtain flies open and I extend a hand, helping her step out before following her into her room. She heads over to the dresser, picking out a large t-shirt and a pair of black cotton shorts. Darcy pulling those shorts over her hips sans underwear is an image I store for later.

She rests a hand on the dresser for a moment. Fearful the lightheadedness just hit her again, I don't waste time thinking. Reflexively moving across the room to lift her again. Pulling her sage green comforter back, I lay her down and tuck her in. Turning to leave, a small hand grasps my wrist and I pivot back to look at her.

"Stay with me? At least until I fall asleep."

"Let me change out of these clothes." I'm still donned in my white button-up and navy slacks from work today, not having changed before entering her room earlier.

"You've quite literally been inside me. I don't think you need to be modest now." She chuckles, "But if you want, your shirt is on top of the dresser. Just throw that on and lose the pants."

"It's more that I wanted to be comfortable laying in bed." I wink at her, undoing my button-up and placing it where my shirt was. I shuck my pants off and place them with the shirt. I can feel her eyes on me the whole time, making my spine tingle. I try to flex my biceps a little more than necessary.

I slide into her bed with her, resting my back against the headboard and opening my arms to her just as I did a few weeks ago. Holding her is intoxicating. She snuggles into me, slinging an arm over my stomach.

"How are you feeling?" I ask her, keeping my voice low as I rub gentle circles on her back.

"My head is still pounding, but I think the shower and food helped a bit." I feel her smile against my side.

"So, what do you want to do for the gender reveal?"

"I've seen a few viral videos where the parents have a cake made, then they each stick a champagne flute in and lift it at the same time. I feel like that's easy and cute. Plus, we get cake out of it—who doesn't like cake?" She continues, "Then, to share it with everyone we would make the video black and white and change it to color after our reactions so everyone could know if blob is going to be a girl or boy."

"I love that idea. Do you want a boy or girl?"

"Truthfully..." Darcy pauses, briefly. "I don't think I have a preference."

"Yeah. Me either." I imagine a mini version of Darcy running around, and that gives me heart palpitations. I can't tell Darcy no, there's no way on this green earth that I would be able to tell a smaller version of her no.

"I think I need to rest. Thank you for caring for me even though you didn't have to." She says in a gigantic yawn.

"Goodnight Mama." Within minutes her breathing evens out, and I tell myself I need to leave. To go shower and sleep in my own bed, but the lulling of her soft breathing has me closing my eyes and joining her in sleep.

Chapter 13

Sleepy Voices

Darcy ‖ 18 weeks pregnant, October

I wake up to a warm body next to me and one toned, golden arm beneath my head. The other arm is tucked beneath Tatum's head as he sleeps beside me. I know that I told him to go after I fell asleep but I'm glad that he stayed. I find myself studying his features, his dirty blonde hair sticks up in all different directions, his lips slightly parted as snores escape him, and his eyelashes flutter lightly as he dreams. I quietly lean up onto my right elbow to inspect his bicep tattoo up close. A cluster of roses, chrysanthemums, and daffodils sit along his bicep. Roses, I assume because of his mother's name. I'd also venture to guess that the other flowers might be his father's and sisters' birth month flowers. I'll have to remember to ask him.

"Good morning, Mama."

I startle—his eyes weren't open so I assumed he was still sleeping as I ogled him. He chuckles, a deep and throaty sound, "I could feel you staring." They say sleepy voices are sexy but those sleepy laughs sent my ovaries into overdrive.

I brush him off, feeling heat crawl up my cheeks. I can almost guarantee I'm beet-red right now. Tatum's hand comes up, brushing a hair out of my face and leaning into me. Just as luck would have it when I think he is going to kiss me, a wave of nausea rolls over me that I quickly realize is more than that. Jumping out of bed, I barrel into the bathroom and slam the door behind me. Once I am no longer emptying the contents of my stomach into the toilet, I brush my teeth, shower, and fix my hair. Exiting, I find my room empty but see a Gatorade, a scrambled egg, and a piece of toast sitting on my nightstand.

My phone lights up with a text.

TATUM

Sorry that my *almost* kiss made you vomit.

Oh god. Another one pops through.

TATUM

Kidding, I know it was the blob. I had to go change and get to work. I may have slept in later than I was supposed to and was running very late. Sin should be there soon.

I do want to talk about that *almost* kiss later though.

ME

Yeah, of course, Tate. It definitely wasn't the *almost* kiss. Thank you for breakfast.

Another text comes through, only this time from Sin.

SIN

Please tell this doorman I am supposed to be here before I lose my patience and the free massages I was promised for the next year.

I quickly call down to the front, letting him know Sin is supposed to be here, before heading to the entryway to greet my friend.

"Hi, D. Hi nugget." She greets me, then my stomach, wrapping me in her arms before pulling away to look me up and down. Probably taking a physical inventory and mentally checking boxes as she does.

"I'm fine." I involuntarily roll my eyes towards my friend.

"If you were fine, then I wouldn't be here right now." Sin fires back, "I know that you are capable of taking care of yourself, *but* your baby daddy offered to pay for massages for a whole year if I came and Mother Henned you today. Who am I to turn that offer down?"

"Well you're lucky that I've missed you, otherwise I'd be sending you on your way."

"Oh, the drama." She flails her arms in the air for emphasis.

"Who? Me?" I make a show of pointing at myself. "I saw a clip of some new, trashy reality love show, wanna binge it until I decide I need a nap?"

"Now you're speaking my language, let's go." Sin laughs, linking her arm in mine.

We make ourselves comfortable on the black sectional that takes up most of the living room, each grabbing one of my fuzzy blankets. I curl up in what I've deemed my corner, while Sin makes herself comfortable on the other end. I press play on the first episode, immediately knowing we are going to eat this show up.

"Harry is going to go after Isla, but you know she is going to go for Dean and his big dick energy." Not getting any sort of response, I turn to my friend who annoyingly has her nose in her phone like she has for the majority of the episode. "Earth to Sinclair." I snap my fingers, her vibrant green eyes snap up to mine and her fair skin blossoms to a color akin to a freshly bloomed rose.

"Uh, yeah, sorry."

"Sin, were you even paying attention?" I grumble in her direction.

"Of course I was. I think that Dean is going to go for Maya though because she seems unattainable."

"Yeah, but Maya already said she doesn't want anything to do with Dean."

"It's a challenge. Men like a challenge." She raises her eyebrows suggestively at me.

"Who has you so entranced on your phone that you weren't even keeping up with the show?" Sin is not often easily distracted, so whatever—or whomever—has her attention must be important.

"It's no one. Nothing. Everything is fine," she forces, through an uncharacteristic stammer. Sin is very rarely at a loss for words.

"Nope. No way. You're not getting out of this. Tell me." I push. Sin tends to be an open book, so her dismissal is worrying.

"Fine, but you have to promise not to judge me or tell anyone," She gripes. "It's not what you think, okay?"

I mime zipping my lips closed and throwing the key away. "Alright, continue."

"Dom was texting me."

"Like, Dominic Montez, the Manta player?" I do a poor job masking my shock, taken aback by her giving him any sort of attention.

"We all traded numbers for Kodi and Mav's wedding stuff, right? Well, he won't leave me alone."

"Leave you alone about what?" I ask, watching color begin to creep into her cheeks again.

"Nothing, honestly. Just Dom being Dom." She shrugs, placing her phone face down on the arm of the couch.

"Mhmmm," I acquiesce with a hum. "On that note, want to watch some more episodes?"

"Yep, definitely, let's do that."

It's as if she had laser beams for eyes with how focused she is, as we continue to binge our show. We make small comments here and there until I feel myself get sleepy. My eyes get heavier until I succumb to my relaxed state and the softness of the couch.

I WAKE up to my phone buzzing repeatedly beside me, Sin is still with me on the couch, her eyes closed softly as she rests. Flipping my phone, I see that it's two PM and Mom is lit up on the screen. I hesitate in a silent debate about ignoring her call, but despite how upset I still am with my parents, the nagging thought that something has happened to them wins me over. I carefully and quietly exit the living room, padding softly into my room to take the call.

"Hey, Mom."

"Darcy Marie, I thought you had died. I've been calling

for weeks." Her voice is laced with an unmistakable edge of annoyance, and yet not a hint of an apology coming my way.

"I'm aware, Mom, but I've been busy dealing with work and this pregnancy—that thing you wanted nothing to do with."

"I never said that," she dismisses without hesitation.

Of course, she didn't.

"Okay, well, what do you need, Mom?"

"I just wanted to check in and get some info about your baby shower. Have you picked a date for it? How many people can I invite, and have you inked a contract for your photographers?"

I refuse to believe for a moment that her intentions are sincere. She only wants to play the part of the dutiful Grandma. The photographers are so she and Dad can post about it—so not happening.

"Absolutely not, mom. *You* are invited and *you* only. I don't know when or where it's happening yet but if you show up with photographers, they will be asked to leave. And you know what? Let's back up. What is with the sudden change of attitude? When you found out it was a big problem!"

"While your father might not approve, I want to be involved. The photographers are important to document a big milestone such as this."

"Yes, for your socialite friends and the media. Again, Mom, you can attend but if you continue to push then I won't be extending an invite to you at all." Setting boundaries with my parents at twenty-five feels weird, but better late than never.

"Darcy Marie, you should be more aware of the world you were raised in and be grateful for everything your father and I have done for you."

"I gotta go, Mom. I'll text you, bye." I don't even bother waiting for a response before ending the call. As I'm catching my breath, Rose's name pops up on the screen, calling me.

"Hi, Rose," I greet, knowing she can't see my smile but hopeful she can feel it in my voice. She regularly checks in on me, providing constant reassurance when I have a weird feeling, or fear. She has been sending Tate and me little gifts for the blob, adding steadily to the almost-overwhelming pile of things sitting in the soon-to-be nursery.

"Hey Darcy. How are you doing? Do you need anything? Tatum mentioned you had a pretty severe migraine yesterday." Concern is evident in her voice.

"Geez, he's just telling everyone about that, I guess."

"It's only because he cares about you, sweetie."

"No, I know." A wave of guilt crashing over me. "I am feeling better today, but I didn't take care of myself yesterday like I should have—which is how I ended up with the migraine."

"I'm glad that you are feeling better. Your gender appointment is next week right?" She asks, excitement now creeping its way into her tone.

"Yes! And then we will slowly let everyone else know. Immediate family first, obviously." I chuckle.

"Great! I look forward to hearing from you. Love you, Darcy." She always ends our calls or texts by telling me she loves me. Despite this being a normal thing that people do when they care for each other, I find myself struggling to say it back. Even so, she continues to tell me, to let me know she cares for me as if I've always been one of her kids. Like Tatum, and the twins.

"Thanks for checking in. Bye, Rose."

Chapter 14

Truth Be Told

Tatum ‖ 18 weeks pregnant, October

"Nik, just do the commercial. It'll bring you some extra money and attention for the team. You live off of those energy drinks anyways." I sigh, swiping my access card as I jab the elevator button that will take me up to the condo.

"Dude, I don't need the money, and honestly? I couldn't care less if the team needs the attention." Nik's gruff voice comes through the earpiece. These hockey players have had me at my wit's end recently. First, Dom wouldn't do the shelter campaign. I had to force Collins—who is still mad at me for it. Then, Maverick backed out of his energy drink sponsorship because Bella and Kodi have the flu. Now, Nik is avoiding being brought in just to be difficult and for literally no other reason.

"Listen, Nik, I don't care if you need the money or not. You're the captain of the team, so step up and do the ad. I don't have time for this. I'm emailing them right now and telling them you'll be there. Okay, thanks, byeeeeee." I exaggerate that last syllable just to piss him off more then hang up the phone as the elevator doors open to the condo. As I walk towards the living room, I send a quick email to the company telling them how *excited* Niklaus Zaigraev is to be doing the energy drink campaign and how he will arrive promptly at eight AM for the shoot the day after tomorrow.

When I don't find Darcy on the couch, I am headed towards her room but see a blonde, messy bun sitting at the island with a cup of mint tea for her nausea and a book propped open on the countertop. She must hear my foot-steps approach, because she turns towards me as I enter the room, gracing me with a small smile.

"How was your day with Sin?" I ask, pulling Coke from the fridge.

"It was good. Sin and I started a trashy reality show and napped. Your mom called to check in, by the way. A little bird told her I had a migraine yesterday."

I dig into the freezer, pulling out a frozen pizza. I hold it up to Darcy and she nods excitedly.

"Good. I was worried, D," I confide, preheating the oven. Pulling out an assortment of veggies from the fridge, I start to prepare a salad across the island from her.

"I know," she sighs, "I'm sorry that you had to take care of me."

"Don't apologize to me. I want to be here for you but I also need to know you're okay when I'm gone." I still, waiting for her eye contact, my hands halfway through slicing a tomato.

"I know, and I want to be. Yesterday I was just exhausted, and I have started to set food alarms for my naps so I get up and eat." She lets out a self-deprecating laugh.

"You can call one of us to help you instead of being uncomfortable all day," I point out as I resume chopping.

"Me, ask for help?" She laughs, more incredulous this time.

"Mama, I'm serious."

"Ugh, Tate, I know everyone loves me and everyone wants to help and I have to learn to accept it. I get it, okay?"

"Good. Now, do you want cucumbers in the salad tonight?" I ask her.

"No... But." I look up at her to find her smiling brightly at me.

"Pickles?" I laugh. Cucumbers have been hit or miss since she's become pregnant. Pickles, though? Always a yes.

"Pickles." She giggles. Pickles aren't something I typically add to a salad that isn't of the egg or potato variety, but it's a minuscule price to pay if it makes Darcy Whitestone happy.

EATING our dinner on the living room couch, we catch each other up from our time apart. Wanting to talk to her about this morning, I steel myself for rejection. Maybe she doesn't want me.

Maybe all this is, is two separate people destined to raise a child together.

I turn, facing my body towards Darcy, sitting cross-legged in her corner.

"So, about this morning," I start, determined.

"What about it?" She questions, averting her focus to pick at her pilled blanket

"I was going to kiss you."

"I know." She laughs, lightly gesturing towards her

bump that continues to become more prominent as the weeks pass, "but ya know?"

"I do. I'd like to try again." I say, moving a little closer to where she sits, and gauge her reaction. Her cheeks flush. " Kiss you, that is."

"I..." She pauses.

"Can I?"

."Can you?" She raises her eyebrows at me, uncrossing her legs and giving me space to move closer.

"Can I kiss you, Mama?" I'm a hair's breadth away from her face, her breath fanning my face.

"You don't have to ask," she whispers, "You can kiss me anytime you want." Suddenly she tenses, her tone shifting. "Oh my god. I just said that out loud didn't I?" She sounds embarrassed and her cheeks are beet red, it makes me chuckle.

"You did." Before she can respond, my hand is snaking up the back of her neck and pulling her face to mine. Our lips meet softly at first, tentatively touching before she locks her hands around the back of my neck and lays back on the couch, pulling my body down on top of hers. My dick wastes no time, threatening an erection from its position nestled between her legs. She moans into my mouth when my tongue presses against her lips asking for entry, and our kiss becomes feverish. Teeth nip at each other's lips and my hands are tangled in fistfuls of her hair.

I pull back. Unwilling to take this any further tonight. There's no sense in rushing our budding relationship, and I think she's not fully recovered from yesterday. Glancing down, I'm enraptured by her body's visceral reaction—her swollen pink lips, the way her breathing sounds slightly elevated, how her cheeks are still rosy, and her brown eyes thirst for mine.

"You're breathtaking."

"I'm a literal mess. I haven't even brushed my hair today." Her eyes crinkle in the corner as she giggles.

"You're right, let's get those off you for a better look" is what my cock encourages me to say but after silently telling it to shut up I say something more polite.

"My point still stands." I smile down at her, I've somehow managed to hold my weight off of her stomach this whole time but my abs are starting to cramp and if I stay in between her thighs any longer, I may end up going back on the fact that I don't want to rush us. I pull myself up into a sitting position bringing her with me so she's nestled into my side.

"Let me take you on a date, Darcy." She turns her head up to look at me, a grin planted on her beautiful face.

"I want to say yes but I'm scared."

"Why?" Genuinely wondering what she means.

"Kissing you is one thing but going on a date feels like cementing something and I don't know what that something is."

"Darcy," I sigh. I want her to know this isn't just me trying to get in her pants or trying to force her into a relationship. "I've had feelings for you for a bit now and we've been spending time together. Truth be told, I've always been attracted to you. Not just your body but your entire personality. We can take it one day at a time, but right now I'm just asking if I can take you on a date. Maybe we decide to stick to co-parenting or maybe we decide to do this together. Either way, I'd like to explore my feelings for you and continue getting to know you better—when you're feeling up to it."

She's silent for a beat, taking in everything that's just

poured from my heart. "I'd love to go on a date with you Tate."

"Yeah?"

"Yes." She smiles up at me and I place a kiss on her forehead.

"Do you want to watch some Gilmore Girls before bed?"

"Wait, what?" The surprise is evident in her tone, her eyebrows meeting her hairline and lips parted in a small o.

"I've been watching, trying to catch up so we can watch together."

"Why would you do that?"

"I wanted to spend more time with you. It was one of the ways I could think of. I think I'm caught up, according to Netflix at least."

"Let's do it. First though, team Dean, Logan, or Jess?"

"At this moment, Jess."

"Good answer."

Chapter 15

Jules and Julia Co.

Darcy ‖ 19 weeks pregnant, October

I don't know why I'm so nervous. It's not like finding out the gender of our child is going to change anything but for some surprising reason, my body is thrumming with anxious energy.

Tatum parks the car in front of the office before coming around and opening my door, taking my hand in his once I'm out of the car. "Ready?"

"As ready as I'll ever be." He squeezes my hand reassuringly.

Once inside the office, I check in and we take our seats waiting to be called back.

"Darcy." A nurse calls me back finally... My bladder is absurdly full. The nurse does all of her routine checks before getting us settled into a room while we wait for the tech. We sit for a few moments in silence before there's a knock at the door and Penny, the same ultrasound tech from our first appointment, greets us with a smile.

"So today's the big day, huh? Gender day!" She's got

exuberant energy as if this is her favorite part of the job, which admittedly sounds pretty fun.

"We're excited to know, but it's a secret for now! Can you just place the gender in an envelope for us?" I smile back at her.

"We feel ready," Tatum adds.

"Alright, lean back, and let's get this show on the road." Penny places the cool jelly on my stomach, smoothing the wand over my stomach for a few moments before the steady heartbeat of our baby sounds in the room. "Give me just a moment to find a position where their genitals aren't in the shot so you can see your little one."

She adjusts the positioning of the wand putting more pressure on my bladder, before turning the screen to us. The baby doesn't look so much like a blob anymore. There's a clearly defined head, two little hands, and hopefully two little legs. Even if not, this is still the most precious baby I've ever seen.

"Um, does the baby have two legs?" I blurt. Penny chuckles but Tatum looks flabbergasted by my outburst. "I'm sorry I just saw the arms and I was wondering if the bottom half looks healthy."

"Your baby does appear to have all its limbs and you'll be able to see each one of them in the gender photos. I'm going to turn the screen back, capture a few images, and get those squared away for you. You should come in twice more before you reach twenty-eight weeks, at which point we will have you come in every two weeks until weeks thirty-eight through forty. If you make it that far, you'll be coming in once a week until labor," Penny explains to us, while she busies about behind the monitor. Before long she's made short work of cleaning my stomach, helping me into a seated position. After the first few appointments, I learned that leggings and baggy shirts are the go-to outfit because it's unrestrictive and super comfortable.

"Thanks, Penny, I'm sure we will see you again soon." Tatum nods in her direction as she walks us back to the waiting room. I gave her a small wave before stopping at the restroom then reception to schedule my next appointment.

Tatum waits by the front door, opening it for me before walking beside me across the parking lot.

"The blob's little face is so cute," I gush, "I wonder if they will look more like you or me."

"I think if we have a little girl, I would be in a lot of trouble between the two of you." He chuckles as he pulls the passenger door open, my heart beats a little faster at his admitting that.

"I don't know if I should be offended or not," I toss in his direction as he circles the car, sliding in behind the steering wheel.

"You shouldn't be, it's not a bad thing. Ready to go get a sweet treat?" He flashes me his bright smile.

"Yes, please. Sweet treats sound wonderful." I grin back at him. Tatum starts the car, heading in the direction of the bakery.

Tatum called this small, charming mom-and-daughter-owned bakery, *Jules and Julia Co.*, sometime after we decided to use a cake for our gender reveal to see if they could have a cake ready for us the next day. They were so excited that we chose them to create our cake for us and took down all the details. Small vanilla cake, white icing on the outside with pink or blue icing on the inside.

When we arrive, the bakery is quiet aside from soft pop music coming from the back. A pervasive aroma of freshly baked cakes, vanilla, and chocolate batters dance with the smell of strawberry and orange compotes in perfect symphony around us causing my stomach to growl.

"We'll grab lunch on the way home," Tatum states as we approach the register and ring the small bell placed there.

"Good afternoon! How can I help you?" A woman who can't be more than twenty years old asks as she rounds the corner, her apron covered in what I assume is flour and icing, some even on her forehead.

"I called last week about a gender reveal cake. We just had our appointment, I want to drop the results here and go ahead and pay for the cake." Tatum tells her, leaving me to inspect the glass display full of treats including fudge, brownies, chocolate chip cookies, and cupcakes.

"And add on whatever she wants as well, please." He tacks on with a wink.

"We have some seasonal items towards the end of the case." The young woman tells me and *obviously,* now I am headed towards that end of the counter eyeing my options. She and Tatum chat for a few more minutes quietly and I decide on a hunk of peanut butter fudge and Tatum chooses a salted caramel cookie.

"Thanks again, Julia. We'll see you in the morning, have a good rest of your day."

Chapter 16

Morning Daddy

Tatum ‖ 19 weeks pregnant, October

Six in the morning, the bakery doesn't open for another hour yet and I don't know what to do with myself. Darcy was still sleeping soundlessly when I peeked my head into her room and I intend to let her rest until she wakes up on her own. I throw on jeans and a white shirt, throw a black hat on backward because I don't want to deal with my hair and head down to the Porsche.

Once I'm headed towards the local store so I can gather the ingredients to make breakfast I dial Maverick hoping he's up and done with the morning skate.

"Sup man?" Mav says by way of greeting.

"Just going to pick up the gender cake and some flowers. Stuff to make breakfast too. I'm antsy, dude. I was up too early and I didn't want to wake Darcy, so here I am trying to keep myself busy."

"And you decided to call me because?"

"Because you're my best friend and I wanted to talk to you," I sigh.

"You're freaking out."

"I'm freaking out." It should be obvious that since I'm about to find out the gender of my unborn child, I'm feeling a little overwhelmed.

"It'll be fine, man. Though, if you have a little girl good luck, because you'll never be able to tell her no. Fuck, even if you have a boy, you probably won't tell him no either."

"You're probably right. We made out the night before our appointment and I finally asked her on a date."

"No shit, Sherlock. I knew there was more to this than just learning the gender. She said yes?"

"Of course she did. I think I'm already falling for her."

"That's not a bad thing, Tate. Maybe this is life telling you to settle down. With a pretty, strong, and capable woman at that." *Is this life telling me to settle down? Is this my sign that this is what my life is supposed to look like? That I'm supposed to have a family?*

"You're right. Thanks, man."

"No problem. I have to take over Bella duty so I'll talk later. Can't wait to learn about the gender." He hangs up the phone, with perfect timing as I arrive at the grocery store to buy some breakfast ingredients.

EVEN AFTER STOPPING FOR INGREDIENTS, flowers, and a Coke Icee, I arrived at *Jules and Julia Co.* with twenty-five minutes to spare. When Jules sees me waiting in my car, she beckons me in and gives me the cake and envelope before sending me on my way with her congratulations. Returning to the apartment I handle most of the remaining prep work for the grand reveal.

I'm deep in my cooking zone, making some banana pancakes when I hear light footsteps coming down the hallway. Turning, I find Darcy in a messy bun and my t-shirt, sleep lines on her skin where her pillow probably rested.

"Morning, Mama," I say as she approaches the counter beside the oven, leaning back against it as I continue cooking.

"Morning, Daddy." Teasing is evident in her tone but her words shoot straight to my cock. Did we just unlock a new kink? I swiftly turn the oven off and box her into the counter, placing an arm on both sides of her hips.

"Don't call me that unless you mean it," I growl, playfully leaning into her ear and nipping at the lobe. Her chest expands in an unsteady inhale before I continue speaking, "Went and got the cake this morning. Couldn't sleep. Too anxious. You ready to find out what kinda kid we are going to be raising?"

"Yes, but I'm starving and smell bacon. Food first?" She says, wrapping her arms around me and looking up at me with a shy smile.

"Go get dressed, I assume you'll be recording this for the girls which means Mav will see this and nobody gets to see you with no pants on except me." I place a quick kiss on her lips.

She scurries off, throwing in my direction, "Have to video for your family too."

Darcy re-emerges shortly, her blonde hair falling in soft curls around her shoulders. She's put on a light layer of makeup and changed into a white, deep v-neck t-shirt that accentuates her breasts, captivating me. They've grown in the time of her pregnancy and Goddamn do I think about them way more than I should.

While I plate our food, she sets up the camera and we sit at the island, our knees touching as we both quickly eat our breakfast and drink coffee. Silence sitting around us like a warm blanket as we anticipate our gender reveal.

"Let's take some photos first." I'm not big on photos but I know these are memories that we will cherish for the rest of our lives. She has me place my hand on her stomach for a few, we kiss or touch our noses together, and I stand behind her smirking into her hair as she holds the cake out. It feels like it took forever when in reality it took fifteen minutes but it's finally time to find out if we are having a little boy or girl.

"Okay so we will look at each other, and on the count of three press our flutes into the cake. Once both are fully seated, we'll do a second count of three and pull them out. Sounds good?"

I love how the excitement seeps into her tone, her voice a little higher pitched and more rapid than normal. "Sounds good, D."

"Okay, ready?" I nod, and she presses the record button. We get our flutes situated then she counts us in, "One, two, three." We push the cups into the cake and keep our eyes locked on each other.

"You in?" I ask and her giggles make me roll my eyes. "Not what I meant."

"Okay—lift and look on three?" I nod again in confirmation before she counts down, "Three, two, one."

Our hands lift together and see bright blue icing filling our champagne flutes. My heart races at the thought of having a son. My eyes fill with tears and looking at Darcy, I see tears in her eyes, quickly turning into panicked breaths.

I quickly end the recording and pull her into my arms, resting her head on my shoulder.

"Deep breath, Mama. Talk to me. What's going on?"

"We, we are almost halfway through and we aren't prepared at all. Oh my God, we are going to ruin this child."

"Darcy, baby look at me." She gently steps back from me and I take both of her hands in mine. "We can go shopping right now, I'll have the guys over here next weekend putting together shelves and cribs and whatever else we need done. It'll be okay. Kodi has access to the Pinterest board to help me make the nursery of your dreams for our little boy. You're going to be a great mom to our son. Take a breath, we got this."

When she finally calms down she asks me, "Are you happy?"

"So fucking happy." One minute we're laughing and crying over the gender of our baby and the next my lips are on hers and she's practically straddling my lap on this tiny ass island stool. I lift her, heading to my bedroom.

"Let me make you feel good, Mama." Nipping at her neck which elicits another one of those pretty, little moans. "Let me get rid of those racing thoughts for you."

She swivels her hips as I make my way into my room and sit her down on my bed. I force her legs open, stepping between them, dropping to my knees, and pulling her shirt over her head. I reach around, unclasping her bra. When I pull it off her body, her plump tits bounce, eliciting a little groan to escape her lips.

"Are you in pain?" I ask because that wasn't a moan of pleasure.

"They're just a little tender."

"Am I okay to touch them?" I get a feverish nod in response. "Oh, so they are tender and sensitive, huh?" I taunt, leaning into her chest, and taking one full breast in my hand. Gently massaging it, I move to take her other nipple into my mouth.

"Mmm." She moans, her hand tangling into my hair to hold me in place. I swap between them, showing each of her tits some appreciation before I center my hand on her sternum and gently push her backward onto her elbows.

"Can I take these off?" I ask, toying with the button on her jeans.

"Please."

Popping the button with one hand and smirking in her direction causes her to roll her eyes at me. I pull them off, seeing that her nude panties have a wet spot.

"Fuck baby, so wet for me already." I palm myself through my jeans knowing that I am probably going to cum in my pants like a teenage boy touching a tit for the first time, but who can blame me when I have this goddess of a woman laying in my bed, pregnant with my child. I remove her panties. "Put your feet on the edge of the bed and spread that pretty pussy open for me, Mama."

She listens so well, and fuck I can't wait to fully have her again. Feasting on her will have to do for now though. I kiss a trail down her thighs, biting and then soothing it with my tongue. Her hips slightly pushing off the bed with each nip. When I reach her slick center, I blow gently on it causing her to jump and moan.

"Tatum, please." She whines.

"What do you need baby?"

"Your mouth."

"My mouth where?" I look up at her, her pink cheeks and heavy breathing tell me that this beautiful torture is doing exactly what I want, taking her mind off all the things we need to do to prepare for this baby.

"My pussy."

"I love when you tell me what you need."

I let my tongue explore her entrance, licking up and down slowly at first. Darcy's soft mewls fill the room, her body fully relaxing into my bed. I lick and suck at her clit, keeping a rhythm. When her moans get louder, I take my index finger and push into her, rubbing at her g spot in a come-hither motion while I suck her clit into my mouth. Her arousal covers the lower half of my face, and I can't get enough of her warm, slightly metallic flavor. Unable to hold myself back any longer, pulling my dick out with my free hand, being very careful not to lose the rhythm of my tongue. Her hand finds my hair again, and she rides my face. I grow desperate, rutting into my hand with each push into her wet heat. She begins to tighten around me. Her body is arching off the bed and when she screams my name, I cum with her, right there in my hand. The culmination of her soaking my face, her pleasured sounds, and the way she ground into me was too much for me to hold out. I should be ashamed but I'm not. She rides out the rest of her orgasm and then I pull away from her, pushing off my knees and leaning over her to steal a kiss. She goes to grab my cock but I stop her.

"What about you?" She purrs.

"Darcy, I want so much more of this." I push my hand forward, showing her my mess, "that was hot enough to have me coming in my hand. So I think we should go shower."

She chuckles but lets me help her up. We quickly wash off, stealing kisses all the while. Before long, I'm pulling her into my bed beside me—her in one of my Manta Rays tees and myself in low-slung grey sweats. We are going to have to get up and eat lunch soon, but I can't help but place my hand on her stomach where her hand comes to rest atop mine.

"So, do you have any name ideas?" I ask her, breathing in her scent. The smell of my body wash mingling with her fading vanilla shampoo.

"Um, I'm not particularly sold on any but have a few contenders. Quincy, Logan, Noah, and Finn have been ones that have stuck out to me." She says pulling out her phone and opening a list aptly called, "Baby names".

"Hmm, okay. I'm not completely sold on those either, so let's keep workshopping it?"

"I'm open to ideas. I want to decide before he arrives because I saw the cutest sign that we could hang above the crib—it even matches the nursery theme." She smiles as she speaks and I know even if I despise the nursery theme, Darcy is going to get exactly what she wants.

"Can I see the sign and the Pinterest board?" I ask her, excited to see what kind of work she has in store for me and what she's always envisioned for her future children.

"Wait Kodi hasn't shown you?"

"No, she said that I 'haven't earned it' yet, whatever that means."

"She is so dramatic and overprotective." She chuckles, "Can you grab my water out of the kitchen first, please? I'm too comfy here." As if to emphasize her point, she sinks her head back further into my arms, letting her body melt into my bed. I kiss her cheek before untangling my arms and heading to the kitchen. I grab my phone, her emotional support water bottle, and the abandoned, butchered cake for us to enjoy before heading back into the room.

"Oooo you brought treats." She smiles, taking her phone from me after sitting up.

"Of course I brought treats, Mama, now let's see that

nursery. I've been waiting *forever*." I place the cake and forks on the nightstand and slide back into bed beside her, pulling her as close as possible, my arm wrapped reassuringly around her shoulder.

She places her head on my shoulder once again. Unlocking her phone, she pulls up Pinterest and clicks on a board labeled "Baby Reed". This board is meticulously organized into sub-boards labeled, "Maternity Shoot", "Baby Photos", "Birth Plan", "Shower" and "Nursery" along with a multitude of others. For someone who said that we weren't prepared for this baby, I'm amazed at how organized everything seems to be.

"So we know that the beach is both of our happy places and when I found that out, I went straight to Pinterest." Her voice is fast, but not hurried, as she delves into explanation. "This nursery is the embodiment of a beach baby which I think our little Quincy will be." Immediately after trying that name, her nose crinkles and she goes back to her notes app and removes the name, Quincy. "I thought I would like that one, but I don't."

"May I?" I ask, reaching for her phone so I can see the images up close. "I love the idea of a beach nursery since we won't be at the beach house all the time." I take a moment scrolling and clicking on pins up close, as Darcy reaches across me and grabs the cake, nibbling as I look. Pins of a mobile with dangling shells and otters, cream and light sandy wood-looking cribs and dressers, a seashell tummy time mat, some signs with the definition of a beach baby, surfboards, and sea creatures.

"I love it, that mobile is so cute. I think we can use this blue color for an accent wall as well. I think that our little Logan will like it as well." She takes her phone back from me, crossing another name off the list.

"You know if you keep taking names off the list, we won't have any left for him?" I tease.

"We aren't going to know if we like his name if we don't take it for a test drive. You like the theme idea though?"

"I do, I think it's perfect for us and our little guy. But what kind of nursery will he have at the beach house?"

"Oh, there are backup options." *Of course, there are.* "Maybe a dinosaur theme, look how cute these are." I find myself looking through pins of forest greens, dinosaur artwork, sheets, and fake greenery.

"Okay, dinosaurs for the beach house. We *have* to get those dresser drawer handles." Golden dinosaurs replace your typical drawer handle in this particular photo.

"Of course we do." She turns towards me, blinding me with her smile and I can't help but lean in and kiss her for what feels like the fiftieth time today. She tastes sweet like vanilla cake, but the feel of her lips on mine is as natural as breathing, I won't stop unless she makes me. *God, I hope she doesn't make me.*

My phone begins buzzing incessantly on my nightstand, and I can almost guarantee that it's Tinsley or Tessa because we haven't sent the video out yet and reluctantly I pull away from Darcy. Honestly, we haven't even watched it yet. I grab my phone and see it's a video call. I click accept and not only is it either Tess or Tinsley but both of them. My mom is also in the frame, which means my dad must be sitting nearby. I turn my phone to her and she nods for me to pick it up. I make sure we are both in view when all of the excited faces appear across my phone screen.

"OMG, a boy!" Tessa and Tinsley scream simultaneously and with voices full of excitement. Darcy and I look at each other in utter confusion, wondering how the fuck they knew when I see it. Darcy has the tiniest speck of blue icing sitting on the corner of her mouth and how they spotted that is beyond me. I mute us and place my phone face down for a moment, pulling Darcy's face to mine, flicking my tongue out to lick the icing off her mouth, the tiniest moan leaves her lips and I am very glad that I turned the microphone off.

"Got a little icing there." I wink at her before putting my arm back around her and picking my phone back up.

"Well, there's that. Um, surprise I guess?" Darcy laughs anxiously. "I can't believe this is the second time I've ruined a surprise for y'all."

"These are memories that will last a lifetime, it's special and will make the little guy laugh one day or embarrass his future girlfriend." My mom chuckles from the other end of the phone, dabbing at the corner of her eyes with a napkin.

"Congratulations you two." Dad smiles from behind Mom, his arms gently wrapped around her, cocooning her in his love.

"I still want to see the video so I can make fun of Tate for crying." Tessa pokes fun at me, Tinsley joining her in maniacal laughter.

"Remember that when I tell your first boyfriend about your tenth birthday party."

"You wouldn't?!" They scream in unison.

"I would. Don't try me brats." They both huff and Darcy laughs beside me. "But honestly, we haven't watched it ourselves, but once we do and we get it ready, we will text it to you guys."

"Well, we should let you guys make the rest of your calls and enjoy this day together. See you at game night in two weeks." My dad cuts in before we can continue going back and forth like he's always done when we argue.

"Can't wait!" Darcy beams beside me.

"Us either, love you both," Mom says.

"Love you too." We say in unison before ending the call.

"We better get that video out before we receive about ten more of these calls," Darcy says, pulling her phone out. "Oh look, it's already starting. I have thirty messages in the girl's chat and a missed call from Dom."

"Let's watch it together first."

She nods against my shoulder and turns her phone landscape before pressing play on the video. We watch as the realization of a baby boy hit us both and Darcy's panic set in before I abruptly leaned in and pressed stop recording. What happened after is going to live rent free in both of our brains for the rest of our lives.

"Thank you." She says as she begins cutting the video together to make her vision of a reveal video come to life..

"For what?"

"Helping me calm down earlier, it helped."

"Of course, Mama."

"Alright, it's ready." We watch the video again, the video starts with a black and white hue, us laughing as we pull the flutes out, discovering the gender of our baby. It then transitions to color, revealing the blue icing within the flutes.

"Looks great."

She pulls up a text thread with me and sends me the video then pulls up her girl's chat, attaching the video and I see her type, "Not reading all these messages, you impatient hoes, love you."

"Well, that was fast."

"Some of us aren't old men when it comes to the internet. Plus if I want to be an author, I have to learn how to make videos, I've been doing my research," she chides.

"You and I both know that while I may have the know-how of an old man on the internet," I say, turning my head towards her and whispering in her ear, "I'm very proficient where it's important." She shivers in my hold but focuses on the incoming responses from the girls and I send the video to my family and the guys.

DOM

Fucking finally. I've been waiting ALL day for this.

ME

Oh shut up Dominic. It's been a few hours, we were enjoying the moment.

MAVERICK

"Enjoying"

The chat is quiet for a moment as the guys, I assume, watch the video that was sent.

NIK

Screaming and running Elmo gif

NIK

Holy shit, a little man!

COLLINS

I am doing my very best not to scream in Wake, Bake, Repeat right now.

MAVERICK

Congrats Tatum, can't wait for Bella to have someone to play with!

ME

Thanks, guys.

"How are the guys holding up?" D asks from beside me, chuckling at her phone.

"The guys are acting like the guys, but they are happy for us."

"Same, all the girls have sent me photos of them crying." She turns her phone to me, showing me her friends' eyes red with tears streaking down their faces.

"You know I never answered your question that night?" My nerves are kicking up, I know she agreed to go on a date but for some reason, I still have the jitters.

"What night?" She puts her phone down, giving me her full attention as her eyes sear into mine.

"That night of the wedding when you asked if I wanted what Kodi and Maverick have. For a long time, I thought I didn't. That night my answer would have been no, I liked being single and having my personal space. But I know now that I do want what they have. Having you here and us having a baby has changed all of that for me. I know we aren't together but I'd like to be if you'd give me the chance, for you and our son. For us to raise him together as a family, whole and together. So I was wondering if next Friday night, I could take you on that date."

"I would like that." The smile that adorns her face is blinding.

"Me too. Very much." I raise my hands up to bookend the sides of her face, pulling her in for a kiss. It's slow and tender, both of our phones continuing to vibrate on the bed but we are lost in this moment together.

Chapter 17

Spill the Tea

Darcy ‖ 20 weeks pregnant, October

I walk into *The Brunch House* with Sin, Harls, and Kodi in tow. This restaurant was practically made for girls like us, those who love breakfast food and mimosas. It's covered in bright, funky decor, and serves the crispiest hash browns I have ever had in my life. My mouth waters thinking about them.

We managed to pull Harley away from Benji and her studies for the morning, which is good because we can check in with her. She's been distant since Stu's party and our phone call. I've got my date with Tatum next week and I want to have some time with *all* of my best friends before then. Sinclair approaches the host stand and then we are guided over to a small booth on the patio overlooking the ocean.

"D, are you ready for your date next week?" Kodi asks as we get settled into our seats and begin looking over the menu.

"I am." I pause, already feeling my throat tighten, unwilling to admit I'm afraid of getting heartbroken.

"But?" Sin inserts for me.

"But I'm terrified that I'm going to get hurt. You guys know Tate doesn't do relationships and that he never wanted kids. Is he just asking me out and being all caring and kind to be nice? What about me is so special that all of that changed?" Tears begin welling in my eyes as our waitress approaches. Sin orders champagne for the three of them—along with assorted juices and water for everyone. Harley pipes up ordering a raspberry, white chocolate iced coffee before the waitress gives us our space again.

"You know, someone wise once told me that whoever I choose to give my time to was lucky?" Kodi asks, placing a hand over mine on the table.

"And look where that got her." Harley chimes in.

"Tatum knows that we will castrate him if he hurts you or that precious little boy in there." Sin says as she gestures towards my stomach.

"Amen" and "Hallelujah" Ko and Harley call out simultaneously, leaving me unsure of who said what.

"You guys are the best, you know that?" I beam at my friends as they all nod in unison. "So what's going on with everyone else? How's Benji? Ready for your exam?"

"He's great actually." Her curled posture tells me the opposite but I learned after last time not to push her. I see Sin's jaw tick at the response knowing that there's probably more to the story. Harley adds, "I am ready I think and I might have a job lined up at the Right Place, Right Time Center, the one that works with troubled teens where I did one of my undergrad internships."

"That's great! I remember how much you loved learning

there." Kodi adds in as our waitress comes back, dropping off drinks and taking our orders. As if Kodi doesn't eat enough pancakes with Bella, she orders strawberry pancakes with hash browns and a bowl of fruit. Harley orders a smoothie bowl with a fried egg while Sin orders a meat lover's omelet with a small berry parfait. I go with my usual which is a blueberry streusel waffle with a side of hash browns and fruit bowl.

"Alright, Kodi. Spill the tea, how is being married?" Sin asks, Kodi's cheeks redden and I think she's going to spill some sexy little secrets but instead, a choked sob escapes her. I move closer to my best friend, wrapping my arms around her before she has a chance to say anything.

"Oh my god, this is so stupid." She sniffles.

"No, whatever is happening is not stupid. Talk to us." I encourage her, still wrapped around her tightly.

"We had decided that when we got married we wanted to give Bella a sibling as soon as possible. It's only been a few months but it's not happening. It's not to say it won't, which is why it feels stupid."

"It's not stupid at all, Ko. Something that you've always wanted is taking longer than you expected and being frustrated and upset is a normal response. This is something that so many people struggle with and it's okay for you to be feeling this way." Harley soothes.

"I'm trying to be so happy for you, D, but it's been hard, I have to admit." She sniffles again and this time I join her.

"I feel like a shit friend, I've been bothering you about baby stuff and sharing everything this whole time. You've been struggling and I was just rubbing it in your face." The guilt of not being present for my best friend or giving her the support she needed weighs heavily on my shoulders.

"No, Darcy, that's not true at all. I didn't tell you, and it's my responsibility to do that. I should have told you. All of you—instead of keeping it to myself." She hugs me back, tighter this time.

"How can we support you?" Sin asks her.

"I think just being you guys, letting me talk or cry if I need to. Celebrate with me when my body decides it's time. Just don't ask me all the time if I'm okay, I don't think that question will be helpful to me." She says.

We all murmur some sort of affirmation to her before our food is dropped off in front of us. We dig in, silence blanketing us for a moment. Sin is the first to break the silence, "Well I don't have anything fun to share. Just fooling around when work isn't kicking my ass."

"Okay." Kodi claps. "Let's talk about the baby shower."

"Drum roll please." Harley and Sin begin gently tapping their fingers on the table to avoid causing a ruckus in the restaurant.

"The theme is..." I pause for dramatic effect causing my friends to roll their eyes at me. "Baby on Board! So think blues, sandy colors, shells, waves. Everything that encompasses Tate and I's happy place. Tate said we could have it at the beach house!"

Sin mimes a gag, before asking, "I'm assuming you've shared the Pinterest board with all of us?" I give her two thumbs up eliciting another eye roll from her.

"Alright, then we will handle it from here." Harley chimes in, giving the other two a devious grin that I know means they will be going all out for this and I honestly can't wait.

"Are we inviting Lorraine?" Kodi's curiosity piquing beside me.

"I told her she was welcome to attend and would be

receiving an invite but if she causes any problems or shows up with people that weren't invited or cameras she would have to leave."

"Ooooo she's setting boundaries." Harley does a little happy dance across the table.

"I did, I won't let her or anyone treat Hudson the way that she treated me." I crinkle my nose in disgust before pulling my phone out and crossing another name off the list. "Dang it man, names are hard."

"I think once you see him, you'll know for sure what his name is." Sin comments.

"Hmm, you're probably right." The rest of brunch goes by quickly and I head home to take a quick nap before my date with Tatum.

I'M unable to nap when I return to the condo, and Tatum isn't back yet, so I sit at my desk and open my laptop. I open a few tabs including my plotting document, my WIP which I've barely put a dent into, my inspiration photos, my search engine page, and my soft, chill pop mix.

I quickly reread the first couple of chapters I've started, changing quite a few things as I go because it's been almost a year since I've touched this manuscript. The story I'm planning to write follows a small-town girl, Reese, who moves to a big city and begins working for grumpy, million-aire Trent as his architecture assistant. We've got fake dating, a small-town girl and a big-city guy, and my personal favorite, grumpy and sunshine.

Two hours and two thousand words later, I hear the

front door click and quickly move out to the living room hoping Tatum is up for some cuddles.

"Hi, Mama." His face morphing from stoic to joy when he sees me lying on the couch.

"Hi, cuddles?"

"Please, just let me get changed." Tatum places a quick kiss on my lips before heading to change.

Laying in his arms with his hand resting on my stomach feels as natural as breathing.

"What's your favorite movie?" He asks, breaking the peaceful silence between us. His thumb moves slowly along my bump awaiting my answer.

"Hmmm, it depends on my mood. If I want a classic, 10 Things I Hate About You is a go-to. If I want something emotional, I'd probably go for A Walk to Remember. Something silly, probably Shrek-the movie of my childhood." Tatum chuckles at that last one, his hot breath fanning my neck and sending tingles between my legs. "What about you?"

"Probably World War Z. I love a good zombie movie. Favorite color?"

"Aquamarine, you couldn't tell?"

"Of course I could, I just wanted confirmation. I know your favorite food is lasagna and your favorite flower is a lily. My favorite color is green and my food is my mom's pot roast."

"Her roast is to die for." I laugh and turn to face him, letting my head rest along his bicep. "What do your tattoos mean?"

"Well, the rose is for mom. The chrysanthemum is dad's birth flower and daffodils are the twins."

"I thought so, I just wanted confirmation." I throw his

words back at him before my stomach causes me to jolt. Tatum's brows dip in concern. "I'm... I'm okay. I think the baby moved?" Whatever it was, it felt like popcorn popping.

"Are you serious?" Just as he asks, it happens again.

"Yeah, give me your hand." His hand that was wrapped around my back moves towards my front. I guide him to where I felt the movement, pressing his hand in with my own. We stay there, eyes locked on one another, waiting. After a minute or two, it happens again and Tatum's eyes light up. Excitement now written across his features where concern previously was.

"That was so weird but also so fucking neat." He smiles at me.

"It was, wasn't it? I'm glad you got to experience it with me." I lean up, placing a gentle kiss on his lips. At this moment, I'm genuinely thrilled that Tatum is here with me. Not just the baby moving but this whole pregnancy and what's to come for us. He's been nothing but attentive, kind, and caring with me. Making sure I'm fed, have a place to stay, and a way for me to do my dream job.

"Me too, I know that this isn't exactly what we expected our lives to look like right now. But I am happy that these little milestones are ones that I'm getting to have with you." He says, continuing to mindlessly rub circles on my stomach where the blob was moving around. The baby's movements seemed to slow with Tatum's touch, similar to how my heart calms in his presence.

"I can agree with that, I didn't think I would be pregnant at this point in my life. Nor did I think I would have left my job, ever really."

"I didn't think I would've gotten somebody pregnant, but I have to tell you that I'm pleased it was you."

"Honestly, I could say the same."

This time, Tate is the one leaning down to kiss me. " Want to watch some Gilmore Girls before dinner?"

"Yes please." The rest of the night goes by in a flash, stealing kisses, talking theories about our show, and cuddling on the couch.

Chapter 18

Pottery and Pasta

Tatum ‖ 21 weeks pregnant, October

Darcy emerges from her room at six PM on the dot, her blonde hair is curled and the top half is pulled out of her face—her makeup a little heavier than normal, covering up that freckle I adore. Her bump is accentuated by a cream-colored skin-tight dress with a forest green cardigan covering her arms and shoulders. I'm on my feet and closing the space between us without a second thought. My hands find her hips, gently pulling her body to mine. "You are so beautiful."

I watch as her fair skin pinkens from the chest up before she practically whispers, "Thank you."

"You ready?" I ask her planting a kiss on the top of her head.

"*Yessir*. What are we doing?"

"It's a surprise, I think you're going to love it though," I tell her, after taking her clutch and interlacing her fingers with mine, guiding her into the elevator and getting her tucked into the car. She hums along to the radio as we make the drive to *Potters, Painters, and Pasta.* It's a craft venue that recently opened and when you're done with your art, they have a small Italian restaurant attached. I hope that Darcy enjoys my choice of location, I didn't want to tell her because I felt like if this place was on her radar, she would have been here fifteen times by now with the girls. Selfishly, I wanted her to experience this with me for the first time.

"What is this place?" She questions as I park the Porsche in front of the building.

I turn to her, explaining, "I saw this video online where this couple found out they were pregnant and decided that for their child's birthdays, they'd paint him a plate with all the different things that he'd enjoyed throughout the year. On his eighteenth birthday, he would have a full selection of plates as keepsakes of his childhood. I know our little man isn't here yet but I thought it would be cool to go ahead and start from age zero, maybe introduce him to us and the things we like. Plus afterward, they have a small Italian restaurant that we can grab food from."

For a moment she doesn't say anything and it makes me second guess my decision, "You know maybe this was a stupid idea, we can just go grab dinner somewhere else if you want."

"No, Tatum." Darcy's small hands grab mine, "I love it, this was so well thought out and well I just don't know how to respond." My chest loosens a little, easing my anxiety over my choice.

"How about a thank you kiss? Then we go inside so we don't miss our time slot." I smile at her and her lips are immediately on mine. Gentle and soft, I can feel her gratitude seeping into the way her lips touch mine, the way that her body leans into mine, soft and pliant. I need to get her out of my car before I turn us around and keep her in my bed all night. Reluctantly, I pull away, her cheeks rosy and eyelashes fluttering slowly as if the kiss shook her. "Let's get inside before I cancel our reservation and take you home."

"Not until *after* we paint pottery and eat pasta. Little man wants breadsticks." She smiles, waggling her eyebrows at me.

I hop out of the car, extending my hand to assist her once I've reached the passenger side. Once she's out, I intertwine her fingers with mine and we walk in.

There's a young man, probably around twenty-two sitting at the front desk, reading a book, bright blue hair sits atop his head. He notices us, snapping his book shut before saying, "Welcome to Potters, Painters, and Pasta. Do you have a time slot reserved tonight?"

"We do, it's under Tatum Reed." He looks at the computer then at me then back to the computer. The smells of paint and marinara sauce mingle in the room, I find it weirdly comforting.

"Found you. So behind me, you'll see the pottery pieces to choose from, once you've decided the one that you want, you'll head to that corner." He gestures towards the far side of the room. "And Zoey will get you set up with whatever colors that you want to use. Once you've got it painted, you'll take the piece back to Zoey, then go through those double doors and they'll get you set up with dinner. You'll pay for everything on your dinner tab, just give them this ticket and we will call you once your piece is dried, fired, and ready for pickup." He smiles, effectively dismissing us. There are no other customers and pop music plays softly throughout the room. I pull Darcy in the direction of what looks to be dinnerware, inspecting and choosing a plate.

"Should we do a beach theme? Sand and water, shells,

maybe lasagna, and a Coke Icee?" Darcy asks as we head to meet Zoey at the paint station.

"I love that idea, let's add in a hockey puck because you know little dude will be on skates as soon as he can stand if it's up to Uncle Dom," I retort, approaching the young woman, her onyx hair held back by chopsticks.

"Hiya, what colors are we looking at today?" Zoey asks with a bright smile on her face. Darcy proceeds to rattle off the colors she believes we will need, I toss in a forest green and aquamarine as well. Zoey hands us the plate of colors with another one of her chipper smiles.

"Let's sit over there." Darcy gestures towards a booth tucked into the side of the room, red plastic lines the seat and it gives us plenty of room to set the plate and paints down between us.

"Okay, where should we start?"

"I'm thinking waves then we add in all the personal touches like the Icee and hockey puck. What do you think?"

"That's a great idea. Are you an artist along with being an author?" I ask, receiving a full-blown cackle.

"*Aspiring* author and absolutely zero artistic bones in my body." She emphasizes aspiring, as if writing a book isn't a big accomplishment, before beginning to spread a darker blue onto the pottery piece—I join in with a lighter attempting to give some depth to the waves.

"Baby, writing a book is a really big fucking deal. Even if it never sees the light of day, which it will, you did the fucking thing and that is something I will make sure you are incredibly proud of every day for the rest of my life."

"I appreciate your support and willingness to help me accomplish my dreams. It means a lot to me, Tatum." I can see her cheeks lift as she smiles softly down at our plate which honestly doesn't look terrible.

We continue working on the plate for baby boy with my final touches including an attempt at the birth flowers of his future family, a book for his Mama, and a smiley face because I hope our little man's life is full of life and laughter. Light conversation flows between us before heading over to indulge in pasta.

Our drive home was filled with a tranquil silence, my hand had a firm grasp on Darcy's thigh the entire way and I enjoyed the way she squirmed beneath my grasp.

"I ate so much pasta. I don't know how there's any more room for the baby in there." She sighs contentedly as I pull into our parking spot.

"That linguine was to die for, definitely going to have to make another trip."

"Good thing we have eighteen more excuses to go back!" Her laugh fills the car before she steps out, meeting me at the hood.

"That we do," I say as I approach her, pulling her into me and in for a kiss. She immediately opens up for me, deepening our connection. Her hips grinding into mine and fuck I can't get enough of her. "You better stop that before I bend you over the hood of the car."

She pulls back breathlessly, "Under different circumstances, I wouldn't complain about that but the bed sounds better. Let's go."

Holy fuck, I don't think my dick could get any harder than it is now. She scurries away, guiding me towards the elevator, swiping her key card with so much fervor that I'm worried for her joints.

"Slow down Mama." I grab her waist, pulling her ass against my front, "We have all night." Her body relaxes into mine, the elevator dinging as we pass each floor. I can't help but move one hand to the hem of her dress, barely caressing the skin beneath it.

"All night sounds like a long time, think you can handle me that long?" She's not facing me but I can see the sly grin that spreads across her face in the mirror of the elevator. I find myself gripping her hip and continuing to tease her to avoid taking her against the elevator wall.

There's a ding then Darcy is jamming the up button and all but dragging me down the hallway towards my bedroom, tossing her clutch and losing her shoes along the way.

"Baby, what has got you so worked up?" I trail behind her, chuckling at her enthusiasm.

"I don't know, pregnancy hormones or something. I just want you, Tate. Enjoy it before the celibacy phase hits." She turns, smirking at me as she slides her cardigan off her arms and begins sliding her dress up and over her body. She crawls into bed, blonde hair fanning out over my pillows, chest rising and falling, eyes fixed on mine as she waits for me to join her.

No one told *me* there would be a celibacy phase *but* I'll do it for her.

"Well, in that case, get comfortable." My clothes come off just as quickly as hers and I'm pushing her legs open, groaning at how wet she already is and I haven't even touched her yet. "Fuck me, you're soaking already."

"Tatum." She squirms beneath me, as I continue to peruse her naked body. Her nipples taught, her bump blossoming full of life, and her hands placed over mine where I spread her open, "Please fuck me."

"I want you to cum for me first, Mama."

"Trust me, that is not going to be a problem." The blush of her skin darkens, creeping down her chest, "please."

"Whatever you want, Darcy." I move to my knees, stroking my dick which causes her to squirm beneath me some more, attempting to get the friction she so badly needs. Rubbing my cock through the slickness between her legs, she whimpers, attempting to lift off her hips but I hold her still.

"It's coming Mama, be patient." I push my cock into her inch by inch, her breaths caught in her throat. Watching her chest rise and fall, her fingers pinching her nipples, her stomach plump between us, and fucking hell she looks so good pregnant with my child, "I'm going to put a baby in you."

"I'm already pregnant, Tatum." Her giggle quickly turns into a moan when my fingers find her clit.

"Yes, but, Mama, seeing you so full of my seed is so fucking hot that I am definitely getting you pregnant again." She gasps and I let my free hand move over her stomach as I continue to push in and out of her, feeling her clench around me.

"Fill me up then, Daddy." Those are the last coherent words she gets out because as they fall from her lips they let loose a monster inside me I didn't know existed. I drill into her, and her screams of pleasure ricochet around the room along with the sound of my bed frame banging into the wall.

"Fuck me, you feel so good. I'm going to fill you up until I'm spilling out and then I'm going to do it again. You'll be carrying my children over and over again." She nods fervently, another orgasm ripping through her, causing wetness to gush over my pelvis and her thighs, sending me over the edge with her. I lean into her, kissing her softly before pulling out, some of my cum coming with my cock. I let my fingers scoop it up and push it gently back into her, she wriggles a little but doesn't complain about the move, "Can't lose any of that."

After getting us both cleaned up, I pull Darcy into my arms and sleep takes us both.

LIKE I DO MOST WEEKDAYS, I'm up at five AM, I don't even need an alarm anymore. My body just wakes up, something isn't right though. My left side is empty and cold where it should be warm and have Darcy wrapped around it as she has been since our date Friday. Letting my body stretch, I roll out of bed throwing on a t-shirt and socks that I grab from my dresser before peeking my head into her room. She's crouched over her computer, and the sounds of keys furiously clacking along with soft music fills her room.

I approach her quietly, wrapping my arms around her from behind and reading over her shoulder.

"Hey! No sneak peeks... yet." She quickly minimizes her writing software before turning to me.

"Why are you up so early?"

"Couldn't sleep," She shrugs. "Decided to get some writing done since I will more than likely be taking a nap this afternoon during my normal 'working' time."

"That's smart of you, babe. I'm going to hit the gym at the arena and then go wrangle some hockey players. Call me if you need anything. I'll see you later." I guide her chin up to plant a kiss on her lips before heading out.

The first half of the day goes by in a flash and now I'm sitting with the guys in the cafe arena eating lunch. We have a meeting in a bit to discuss upcoming team fundraisers and wanted to eat beforehand. Conrad walks by our table glaring like he wasn't invited to join us before plopping at a table on the opposite end of the seating area.

"How's Darcy doing?" Collins asks, dipping his fries in mayo like a psychopath.

"Dude seriously, can you like mix that with something?" Dominic groans, he almost looks like he might turn green.

"No, it's perfect the way it is." Collins replies, "Anyways Tate, you didn't get to respond."

"She's good, was writing when I left this morning. I took her out last week."

"Like out... on a date?" Nik pipes up, eyebrows pinched together in confusion.

"Yes, yes he did." Maverick claps a hand on my shoulder, "Our little guy is growing up."

"You are so lucky I have to act professional here. Just know I'm mentally flipping you off right now." The table breaks out in laughter, grabbing the attention of a few passers-by but it doesn't stop my best friends from laughing at my expense.

"Haha, I get it. I caught feelings for her, okay? I plan to continue pursuing this as long as she will let me." I admit.

"We are happy for you, she's great. Plus because Kodi and Darcy are basically sisters, we will be like brothers-in-law." Maverick chuckles from beside me but the mention of marriage has me feeling this weird mix of excitement and nerves inside my chest. *Would she consider marrying me? Is she willing to fully give her heart to me, the guy known for chronically avoiding relationships?*

Speaking of Darcy, my phone begins to buzz on the

table. A photo from our private gender reveal popping up in front of me. "I've gotta grab this, I'll meet you guys in the boardroom."

"Hey Mama, what's up?" I answer as I walk in the opposite direction of the guys to get some privacy.

"Okay, so, don't freak out." There's an uneasiness in her voice that has me moving a little faster and towards the exit doors of the arena.

"What's wrong? I'm on my way."

"Nothing I just maybe, possibly, probably for five minutes thought I was going into labor."

"Darcy, what the fuck? Why are you not heading to the hospital?"

"Because I talked to both Rose and the doctor and they said I'm experiencing Braxton Hicks then I took a nap once they calmed down." She chuckles on the other end of the phone.

Wait... She called my mom because she was worried that she was going into labor. My heart pinches in my chest, warmth blooming over the fact that she would call her in such a nerve-wracking situation.

"What are Braxton Hicks?" I ask, my nerves settling somewhat now that I know she is okay.

"False labor pains—as long as they don't get closer together, or grow more intense, we don't have to worry." She pauses, "Tate, I promise I'm okay. You don't have to worry about me but I wanted to tell you."

"It's my job to worry about you." We sit with my statement for a quiet moment before I check my watch and realize I need to get upstairs, "I have to get to my meeting but call if you need anything. I won't hesitate to walk out of this building for you."

"Thank you, Tate. I'll see you later, bye."

"Bye Mama." I spend the rest of the afternoon distracted, wondering if Darcy is okay at home. When five PM hits, I don't stop to chit chat, don't grab my afternoon pick me up, I bolt to my car and get home to my girl.

Chapter 19

Stay Wild My Ocean Child

Darcy || 25 weeks pregnant, November

After my mental breakdown over us not being prepared to welcome our baby boy home, Tatum and I spent an afternoon curating an online cart of everything we need and want for both nurseries. Over time, packages slowly started showing up and now everything is here. We've been getting to know each other better, going on more dates, binge-watching Gilmore Girls and I'm a quarter of the way through my first draft of my debut novel.

Dom, Harley, Mav, and Kodi should be here any minute to help us put everything together, we got lucky that they are playing at home for Thanksgiving week. Last weekend, Nik and Collins came and painted with Tatum. They wouldn't let me step foot in the room until it aired out but now I stand here taking in the cream walls with the one accented in the shade "blue grotto" envisioning what the room will look like once it's put together.

"Mama, everyone is here." Tatum softly says from the doorway, catching me off guard.

I turn to him and he graces me with a soft smile that I return. "I didn't hear you come in."

"You seemed pretty deep in thought." He steps into the room and I meet him there, wrapping my arms around his neck, and letting my forehead rest on his.

"Just admiring the handiwork I wasn't allowed to witness last weekend."

"We had to protect you D, you know that."

"I do, but you know I like to be doing things."

"Well, now you can do one of your favorite things, tell people what to do." He winks at me then places a soft kiss on my lips, I don't want it to end and it seems like Tatum doesn't either so we stand in the middle of our son's room kissing until someone clears their throat from the entryway. We separate, Tatum's cheeks and I'm sure mine tinted pink as we turn to our friends.

"Besties!" I squeal as Kodi and Harley push their way past Maverick with ease which is surprising considering he has, at minimum, a foot on each of them. Bella follows behind them.

"Besties!" I hear Dom mock our squeals as he enters the room opening his arms to Maverick and Tatum who surprisingly join him as they jump and spin together in a little circle.

"We love these guys?" Kodi chuckles in my ear.

"We do Mama," Bella screams up at us causing me to chuckle.

"You love one of them, I'm falling for the other, and then there's Dom," I whisper so only she and Harley can hear me.

"Holy shit. Did you just admit that?" Harley gasps, pulling back, grabbing my head, and turning it back and forth as if she is checking for injuries.

"I did, now let's get to work, hoes. I've got a kid to prepare for."

"Where can we start?" Maverick asks.

"The men are on furniture duty. Everything that needs to be put together is on that side of the room," I gesture to the opposite wall, "Once it's together Tatum knows where we want them to go. Ladies, we are going to start putting away what we can until things are put together or ready to be hung."

"Alright everyone bring it in." Dom pipes up.

"Bring it in?" Tatum quirks a brow at him.

"Yeah, we have to put our hands in the middle and break," Dom says—like it's an obvious thing for us to do.

"Um okay, I guess." Harley heads towards the center with Dom and then we all file in, our hands piled in the center.

"On three... Baby Reed." Maverick says, scooping Bella up so she can be part of our circle.

"One... Two... Three." Then in unison, we chant "Baby Reed" and get to work.

"Bella, what movie do you want to watch?" Maverick asks Bella, but if I know anything about Bella she isn't going to watch a movie while we work.

"I don't want to watch a movie, I want to help." Over the past year and a half, she has gone from speaking in broken sentences to full ones and it still makes me a little teary-eyed watching her grow up.

"How about you help Mama, Auntie Harley, and Auntie D?" Kodi smiles down at her with such adoration, I wonder if this will be how Tatum and I are when our little guy arrives.

"I'll help Auntie D with baby's stuffs." Bella beams at me.

"That sounds so fun, Bella Bear. I can't wait to show you all the outfits we've picked out for your new friend." I can't help but grin at her and when I look up Tatum is watching me with what feels like adoration in his eyes.

"Damn it, Dom, hold the leg still so I can screw it." I hear Maverick growl ten minutes later as the girls and I are oohing and aahing over the cutest set of bamboo pajamas covered in bats and ghosts.

WE SPEND the rest of the day organizing the nursery before feeding everyone tacos and sending them on their way. Now we are sitting on the floor in the room, Tatum's arms wrapped around me from behind, and my head rests against his chest as we take in our handiwork.

The closet sits on one side of the room, home to all of his newborn clothes on hangers. The dresser sitting inside beneath his clothes—holds his extra onesies, diapers, and an assortment of other newborn care needs. His crib is pushed against the wall opposite the entryway, sitting next to the sand-colored rocker that I picked out from the furniture store—it's equipped with a cup holder and phone charger. It even reclines for the nights we have to snuggle him a little longer. The wall across from the closet sits his bookshelf, holding a few of our childhood favorites such as Goodnight Moon and The Very Hungry Caterpillar. After the shower, it will probably be overflowing as we've asked people to bring signed books instead of greeting cards. The changing table is stocked and ready next to it.

"Is it everything you wished for?" Tatum asks timidly, almost as if he's worried that I hate it.

"Ugh, this turned out perfect." I sigh happily, squeezing Tatum's hand that's resting over mine on my stomach. "You know my favorite part?"

"Tell me."

"It's unique to us." I turn my head to look at him, finding that he is already looking towards me.

"I love that, too." He kisses me slowly.

"The sign too, it's so cute above his crib." I gesture towards the wooden letters that spell out 'Stay wild my ocean child' against the blue wall.

"He is going to be an ocean child."

"Have you met us? Of course, he is."

"Hey, Mama?"

"Yeah, Daddy?" He growls from behind me at that.

"Before we go to bed, can I read him a story?" He pauses, "Mom says Dad read to her stomach every night so that we would recognize his voice when we were on the outside."

"I bet he would love that. Can we do Goodnight Moon?"

"Of course we can but first I want to kiss you again."

"Please do." I chuckle as Tatum takes my lips again before standing and grabbing Goodnight Moon off the shelf. I move to the chair and Tatum kneels on the floor beside me.

"In the great green room..." Tatum begins, I let myself get lost in the soothing tone of his voice as he reads to our son.

When he's finished, he places a gentle kiss on my stomach, helping me up and guiding me to bed where exhaustion settles in quickly. Tatum's warmth and breathing lull me into the best sleep I've had in weeks.

Chapter 20

There's That Fucking Panic Again.

Tatum ‖ **25 weeks pregnant, November**

"Oh my god, this apple pie is the best thing that I've ever put in my mouth." Darcy moans around her fork as we sit at my parents for Thanksgiving lunch.

"That's because you haven't had something else in your mouth yet Mama," I whisper in her ear, across the table from my bickering sisters. She chokes on her bite, scrambling to gulp water down, and her face turns beet red.

"Tatum you can't say things like that!" She slaps my arm lightly.

"I'm twenty-nine years old, I can say whatever I want." I give her a mischievous grin.

"Do you guys have time for a game of Trouble?" Tinsley asks from her seat, hope blooming behind her eyes and I check my watch before nodding at them. Darcy and I have Friendsgiving after this, but there's enough room for a game.

We all migrate to the living space, Tinsley has always played blue, Tessa red, I usually play green, and then mom or dad would play yellow but today Darcy will play the yellow piece.

"Tin, Tess, come here quick." Darcy demands of my sisters, they scramble over the table almost taking the Trouble board off the table, hands outstretched in front of them. My heart warms at the nicknames she's given them over time. "Right here." She takes their hands, slightly overlapping them and pressing gently on the left side of her stomach.

"Holy fuck," Tessa blurts, loud enough for Mom to admonish her from the kitchen.

"Language, Tessa Diane Reed!" Mom calls, a clear warning laced in her tone.

"Omg, this is so cool!" Tinsley squeals, "Does he do that all the time?"

"No," Darcy chuckles, "usually just if he's had yummy food or when I am trying to sleep."

"That's annoying, I need my sleep," Tessa responds curtly.

"So what do you do when you can't sleep?" Tinsley asks.

"I'll write, read, or doom scroll on my phone while listening to your brother snore." Darcy smiles, her cheeks pinkening. In reality, if she can't sleep, she keeps me up all night with her hand wrapped around my cock or my face buried between her legs. Most of those nights end with me buried deep inside of her pussy, while she lays comfortably on her back, fucking her until she's sated enough to sleep.

"Tatum has always been a snorer," Tinsley says behind a laugh.

"Girls stop picking on your brother." Dad hollers from the kitchen, always quick to have my back. Growing up in this house, we've been outnumbered for long enough to learn we only have each other. Now Darcy is added to the picture, leaving us even more outnumbered.

The twins glare at me, and I shrug off their anger with a smug grin, earning me an elbow in the side from Darcy.

"Hey, what did I do?" I grimace rubbing at my abdomen.

"I saw that face," Darcy states curtly and I roll my eyes at her.

"I would *love* for all my children to get along for the rest of the afternoon." My mom admonishes, walking into the room. Dad, hands full of tea mugs joins her to sit on the couch behind the twins, watching us play just like they would do when we were younger.

Their love for each other radiates from all around us. It's in the little things, like the way my dad wraps an arm around mom, still after so many years of marriage, the small smile my mom wears as she watches us, the smell of pie lingering in the air while plates holding only crumbs rest on the coffee table, and the layers of memories that my childhood home holds.

DARCY SNORES SOFTLY BESIDE ME, her hand resting on her lap, wrapped in mine, as I make the drive back into town and towards our best friend's home for Friendsgiving. Soft, contemporary pop music flows through the speakers of the Porsche. Before Darcy, I would listen to dad rock but I'm finding that this music calms me in a way I've never experienced—or maybe it's Darcy's presence. Either way, this music is quickly becoming the new soundtrack of my life.

I park on the road in front of the house, unbuckling myself, then Darcy. "Hey Mama, we made it to Kodi's." I lean in, speaking softly so as not to startle her. She doesn't stir, so I try again. "Darcy, baby, we gotta get inside, everyone is excited to see you."

She moves a little more and I place my lips on hers gently, "Mama, come on. The sooner we get inside, the sooner you can be home and in your pajamas... Well, I guess technically mine."

That is the statement that gets her eyes opening, looking around briefly before gracing me with a smile and kissing me.

"I have to pee," she informs, then she's out of the car and knocking on the front door faster than I can grab the green bean casserole we were charged with bringing tonight out of the back seat.

"What's up, man? How was dinner with your parents? How are they doing, and the girls?" Maverick asks, pulling me in for a hug as I enter his home.

"It was nice, she fits in so well with my family. Like she was meant to be there all along," I say quietly as we walk towards the kitchen.

"Maybe she is."

He says it so casually that it feels almost patronizing. I flash back to where Darcy and I were about six months ago and panic flurries in my chest. In less than three months, I'm going to be a dad.

Will I measure up to the father I grew up with? Or will I fail my son?

"I need to use the restroom, long drive." I abruptly leave

Maverick standing in the entryway to the kitchen, his brows furrowed. I make my way down the hall in a hurry. As I reach for the bathroom door, it swings open, and Darcy pops out looking refreshed from her nap in the car.

"Hi." She says quietly, smiling up at me.

"Hi, Mama." I can hear the strain in my voice, I just need a moment alone to pull myself together.

"Are you alright?" Her beautiful face scrunched up, concern evident in her tone.

"Uh yeah..." I pause, "Just need to use the restroom urgently if you'll excuse me. I'll be out in a moment."

"Yeah... Yeah okay." She still seems confused by my behavior but steps out of the doorway.

"D?" I call, stopping her. I pull her into a hug and kiss the top of her head. She relaxes instantly. After a moment, I release her and she's heading off, down the hallway.

I give myself two minutes in the restroom to pull my shit together and plaster a smile on my face before joining my friends at the dining table. Sitting down beside Darcy, she instantly places a warm hand on my thigh, squeezing it tightly.

"Sorry guys," I tell them, I know they've been waiting on me.

Familiar eyes sit around the table but then I meet three pairs I've only met in passing. Conrad Hoyer, recently transferred to the Manta Rays, sits alongside his girlfriend, Enid, and her younger brother Mace. Mace smiles fondly at Bella as she animatedly tells a story about Shell Shock'd (the rescue Enid works at) and a turtle named Bart.

"Okay." Kodi claps her hands excitedly, "Before we eat let's all go around the table and say something we are grateful for. I'll go first, I'm thankful to have married such a wonderful and loving man." Kodi smiles lovingly at

Maverick who pulls her in for a passionate kiss, which, in my opinion, goes on a little longer than necessary.

"What about Bella?" Bella accosts from Kodi's other side, a finger aggressively wagging in the direction of her Mama.

"Bella, baby, I am so grateful I get to be your Mama every day." Kodi smiles at her, pulling her into her lap as we continue around the table.

"I glad that I get to have pie for dinner." Bella giggles from Kodi's lap.

"With dinner," Maverick corrects with a chuckle. "I'm grateful that my Dad, Grace, and Jason are here, with us, for Thanksgiving this year."

"I'm so happy to be here with my kids, all of them," Stu says, giving us each a smile that has my throat clogged, and I'm not the only one. All of the girls are dabbing their eyes, overcome by Stu's sentiment.

"Jason and I are so grateful that we get to share with you all in person that we will be moving to Florida in December! We closed on our house yesterday afternoon!" Grace's face lights up at her announcement.

"Oh my God yay!!!" Kodi, Darcy, Sin, and Harley scream together.

"Okay, Dom, your turn!" Grace directs.

"I'm thankful for another Thanksgiving where our little family continues to get bigger." He says, Dom may be a big goof but he has a heart to match it.

"You have a surprisingly big heart." Sin says to him, from where she's sandwiched between him and Harley.

"You know what else is big?" Dom waggles his eyebrows at her.

"Do *not* finish that sentence with your niece and my Father at this table, Dominic." Maverick's voice is tight from where he sits causing Dom to wave his hands in a placating manner.

"Well, I am glad I didn't have to work this year and got to spend it with you guys," Sin butts in, taking the spotlight off of Dom—a quick expression of awe passes over his face, like he wasn't expecting her to help him.

"I'm grateful to be graduated and officially an LMHC. Now to do all the supervision hours..." Harley adds quietly.

"You've got this Harls." Collins reassures her before adding, "I'm grateful that we are all healthy and for Precious, my sweet little kitty."

"I'm grateful to play another year with you guys," Nik says. He's getting older and will soon have to retire on his own—or the NHL will decide it for him. Nik gestures to Conrad without saying a word cueing him to speak.

"I just want to say thank you for allowing me a second chance and us to celebrate the holidays with you all." The confidence that I expect from Conrad, dulled.

"Yes, thank you. Mace and I needed a community and you guys have provided it for us." Enid smiles, squeezing his hand atop the table.

"I'm grateful for mashed potatoes and apple pie." Mace, the little smart ass adds, "Your turn, Tatum."

"I'm thankful that Darcy and I have such an amazing support system as we get closer to welcoming our little guy. We can't thank you all enough for everything that you've done." I tell the table and feel D's hand squeezing my thigh again, followed quickly by a kiss on my cheek. A gaggle of oohs and awes ripple out from our friends and family.

"I'm thankful that I have found such a wonderful partner in Tatum throughout my pregnancy. His immense support has gotten me through the hard days and I am so grateful for that." She chokes out, "And the rest of you, you've been great too."

"Anything for you, Mama," I say, driving my point home with a lingering kiss on her lips. She looks at me, eyes wide because I just kissed her in front of our friends. Those big, brown orbs swimming with hope, anticipation, and expectation. *There's that fucking panic again.*

Chapter 21

Friendsgiving

Darcy ‖ 25 weeks pregnant, November

I can sense something swirling behind Tatum's tight facial expression—something that isn't quite sitting right with me. Why is he suddenly on edge, when *he's* the one who just kissed *me*?

Before I can allow myself to spiral, Kodi's voice breaks through the fog, "Well on that note. Let's dig in."

Our meal flies by in a flurry of conversation, and my niggling worries dissipate throughout the evening. Tatum seldom leaves my side, until the guys head out back to play corn hole while the girls and I snuggle up on the couch and talk to Grace about her pending move.

"What made you guys decide to take the jump?" Kodi asks Grace from beside me, her head resting on my shoulder. Bella's droopy-eyed head lies in her lap, the turkey coma and today's excitement slowly starts to sink in.

"Well, we've missed so much of Bella's life already, plus our family is here. This is where we want to be." Grace smiles fondly at the little girl we all love so deeply.

"Too bad you aren't having a girl, D. We were *almost* outnumbering the guys." Sin chimes in.

"You'll have to have a chat with the man who created this," I retort, gesturing towards my stomach. "Regardless, our lil dude is still going to stand up for girl power."

"I know that's right," Kodi says.

"Girl power!" Bella pops her head up, smiling, and we all chuckle in response.

"That's my girl." Kodi laughs, "Time for bed ma'am. Tell everyone goodnight please."

"WELL I DO SAY, good sir, would you like to tell me what happened in there? It seems to appear that your wits were not about you." I ask, as Tatum slides into the driver's seat of his car. There's no need to skirt around the point but I do find myself relying on that silly accent we put on to lighten the mood.

"Tell you about what?" The accent isn't returned, and Tatum's voice is tight, as if he's frustrated that I have the nerve to ask him about his weird as fuck behavior.

"Tatum, don't do this. You were acting weird almost from the beginning and that smile after you kissed me in front of *everyone* was *not* the one you grace me with when you're giving me affection."

"I..." He throws his head back looking up at the ceiling of the Porsche. "I don't even know what to say."

"Don't shut me out. We can talk about whatever is going on. I'm here." My throat threatens to tighten, and the fear that this is getting to be too much for him sits like a lead ball on my chest.

"I freaked out a little bit about everything. Mav asked how lunch with my family was, I realized how well you fit in and when he suggested that maybe you were meant to be there, I panicked. Mav is right though, I do feel like you've been the missing piece." He sighs, rolling his head to look at me. "But, then I got to thinking how we are going to have a child in less than three months and I don't know if I can fill my Dad's shoes. Both in terms of being a parent and being a partner to you. I just got so in my head about the possibility of being a disappointment, especially to you. I'm sorry for making things weird."

"Can you come a little closer? Kind of hard to maneuver with this bowling ball attached to my stomach." Tate laughs lightly then leans closer to me so I'm able to place a hand on his cheek, holding his attention. "Do you remember what I said I was grateful for?"

"I do." His eyes close for a moment, and upon reopening I can see that some guilt and shame swim within. I bring my forehead to his, soaking in his presence and desperately hoping he's doing the same of mine.

"I meant it, you're not a disappointment. I think you were meant to be a father. So when I look at you, and I tell you that with every moment, I fall a little harder, never once having felt alone during this pregnancy. Do you believe me?" The admission sits heavy between us.

Tatum's chest heaves with each breath between us and I find myself holding mine until he speaks. "What are you saying?" He asks, still processing.

"You know what I'm saying."

"Say it."

"I'm saying, Tatum Reed, that I am in love with you." I think if he could pull me any closer, I would be in his lap.

"Love."

The word comes out like a growl but not the bad kind, the kind of sound he makes when I've been teasing him with dirty words or naked pictures in bed while he's working a long day, and he finally gets to come home where I am waiting and ready.

"Yes, I am in love with you."

"Me too."

"You too, what?"

"I love you too. I've never felt such a maddening attraction to someone before you." I don't even have time to respond before his lips are on mine, battling my tongue for dominance. He swallows my soft moan. We stay this way until there's a knock on the window, turning towards the passenger's side, Dom stands there, one of his stupid grins plastered on his face gesturing for us to roll down the window.

"As much as I love a good show, may I suggest you take whatever this is home? You're blocking me in," he elaborates, swirling his fingers at Tate and me in a circle.

"Sorry man. I'm in love." Tatum says, his cheeks are pink so I know that mine are beet red. Dom stands there with his mouth agape, as Tatum rolls the window up and drives us home. We spend the evening wrapped up in each other, whispering words of affection blending with sounds of pleasure until the early morning hours.

Chapter 22

Baby on Board

Darcy ‖ 30 weeks pregnant, January

My feet are so swollen I'm living in my slippers. I feel like a beached whale and I'm supposed to be at the beach house for my baby shower in two hours. I'm about ready to call it quits, giving up on the baby blue maxi dress that I purchased for today—that no longer feels like it fits right—and show up in Tatum's sweats and one of his no-longer-oversized t-shirts because of how big our child is getting.

There's a soft knock on the door and I turn to find Tatum leaning against the door frame, white lilies in hand. Wordlessly, I follow his gaze as it bounces between my tired expression, to the blue dress on the floor. He just waits, knowing that I'll word-vomit any moment. He won't have to wait long.

"My dress doesn't fit like I want it to. My back and my feet hurt. My makeup looks awful and I'm so tired. I don't want to go today." I whine in his direction, squeezing my eyes shut to ward off the tears I can feel burning behind my lids. A warm body and the scent of the sea and cedarwood envelop me, pulling away the tension from my shoulders.

"Do you want to know what I think?" Tatum asks, speaking into my hair.

"I guess." My reply comes out muffled by his t-shirt. His chest moves under my head and a light puff of air ripples through my hair as he laughs.

"That you could wear a damn potato sack and still be the most beautiful woman in the room." He lifts my chin gently so he can hold my gaze, "I think that today is about you, so if you don't like that dress then don't wear it. I think that you should let me see you in it first though."

Tatum lifts the crumpled dress from the ground, gesturing for me to lift my arms above my head. Sliding my arms and head into the appropriate holes he pulls the dress over me and down to the ground before stepping back and taking me in.

"Do a little spin for me, Mama." And because for the life of me I cannot tell this man no, I quickly spin. Suddenly feeling shy, I look to the ground waiting for him to comment.

"You look so fucking beautiful and fuck me if that bump doesn't do something to me." I look up at him just in time to see him adjust himself in his pants.

"Thank you. That helped."

"Good. What shoes are you wearing?" He asks, walking towards my closet.

"White strappy sandals, I think."

Tatum pops out of my closet, my shoes in hand. "Have a seat."

"I can put my shoes on myself, Tatum."

"I know, but I'd like to help you. Once you're ready, I'm going to drive you to the beach house for the shower and

Kodi already told me she would drop you back here afterward." He drops to his knee in front of me, lifting my dress above the ankle, then bringing my foot to his knee and he places soft kisses there before sliding my shoes on. If we didn't have somewhere to be, I would've hiked my dress up even further and pulled his face between my legs. He must know what I'm thinking because he smirks, and tells me, "I've got you later Mama. Let's go."

The drive to the beach house is quick and quiet for the most part. Tatum hums along to the music and I watch the ocean go by, spotting a dolphin or two along the way.

"Ready?" Tate asks, parking the car in front of the house. Luckily the only cars I see so far are Kodi and Sinclairs. Wondering where Harley is, I open my messages and see she hasn't said anything in the group chat.

"Yes, let's get inside before my Mom gets here." Tatum jogs around and helps me out of the car, grabbing my bag including my fuzzy slippers in case my feet start to hurt from the back seat before extending his arm to me.

Near the front door of the house, a small sign reads 'Welcome to Darcy's Baby Shower' and when we enter, nothing seems out of place until we cross the threshold into the living and dining space. A balloon arch sits on one side of the room surrounding a picture backdrop that says 'Baby on Board' and a little tikes cozy coupe that's been painted baby blue sits beside it, complete with a toddler-sized surfboard on top. I take it in, tears prickling my eyes because my friends took my dream and brought it to life. Tatum's strong arms wrap around me from behind.

"They did a really good job."

"They did." Barely holding back the tears, I continue to where the kitchen island is dotted with fruits, charcuterie, little themed cookies that look like the ocean, boards, and seashells along with sand-colored cutlery and plates.

"Ah, you're here!" Kodi squeals, stepping inside from the back porch and beelining it for me. Sin follows not too far behind her, Bella on her hip, and the next thing I know my friends are wrapped around me.

"Do you love it? I put more effort into blowing up those balloons than I've ever done blowing a man." Sin teases while covering Bella's ears.

"Alright, I think that's my cue, can't be late for my Huggies and Chuggies party with the team, whatever that means. Ladies, if I may borrow Darcy for a moment?" Tate asks, clearing his throat.

"Yes, but don't be long. We need to get some photos before everyone shows up!" Kodi says, "Actually, wait. You two stand over there and let us take a few pictures of you together."

We move together to the backdrop where Kodi directs us—in true mom form—giving us comments like "Act like you like each other" and "Darcy Marie give me a real smile" and Sin poses us before Tatum drags me to the front entryway.

"Have fun today, Mama. I'll have sweatpants and an Icee waiting for you at the condo." Tate smiles down at me, pushing a loose curl behind my ear and letting his thumb gently rub the nape of my neck as he speaks.

"I will, thanks for this morning and driving me... and for the lilies."

"Anytime, D." Our lips embrace softly before he leaves and I make my way back to my best friends. Well, two thirds of them.

"Anybody talk to Harls?" I'm trying not to think about

the fact that she promised she would be here and hasn't checked in.

"Nope, she was staying at Benji's last night but told me she'd be here before she went." Sin sighs, resignation is heavy in her tone.

"She hasn't texted?" Kodi asks as she busies herself making sure all, what I imagine are, the final touches are accomplished.

"I'm going to call her." I call her on speaker, knowing Kodi and Sin will want to hear what she has to say if she answers.

It rings and rings and rings until we get her voicemail, "Hey Harley, just checking in. Can't wait to see you today. Love your best bitches."

We don't have much time to sit and wait for a response as the guests begin to arrive. I didn't want it to be a crazy big event. We invited Rose, the twins, my Mom, Grace flew in, and even Enid, Conrad's girlfriend, RSVP'd. She's been hanging out with us more often and since Conrad was taking Mace to the Huggies and Chuggies, I figured she could come to hang out as well, along with a couple other friends and ex-coworkers that I still keep up with.

I'm standing by the snack table, catching up with Quinn, an old coworker, when a shrill voice causes my shoulders to bunch.

"Darcy!" she calls. My mother has arrived.

"Excuse me, it was great catching up with you." Turning towards my Mom, I welcome her, "Mom, glad you could make it."

"I wouldn't miss it for the world, my first grandbaby." She pulls me into a hug before pulling back and inspecting me from head to toe, her scrutiny evident by the way her eyebrows scrunch at my lightly wrinkled dress.

"Lorraine, I'm glad we are finally meeting. I'm Rose, Tatum's mother." This woman is a blessing from heaven, I feel her presence beside me, silently thanking her for interrupting.

"Lovely to meet you." My mom smiles curtly.

"I'm going to let you two get to know one another. Thank you both for being here."

I scan the room for my besties, and when I lock eyes with Sin, she waves me over frantically as if she needs me.

"Doing okay?" Kodi asks, "Did they buy it?"

"Doubtful, but I'm fine. Rose is an angel for taking her attention off of me." I tell them.

"Do you want to do games or gifts first?" Sin asks next.

"Gifts!" Bella squeals.

"Bella baby, the gifts are for Auntie Darcy and the baby in her belly, okay?" Kodi drops to eye level with Bella as she explains this.

"Ah phooey." Bella furrows her eyebrows at Kodi in frustration.

"You can help me open them though." I smile down at Bella, and her mood instantly brightens. She jumps up and down excitedly, running over and plopping down on the floor next to the chair Sin placed near the gift table.

"Alright everyone, let's find a seat, Darcy is going to open her gifts. Tessa and Tinsley, paper and pen for the list are behind you." Kodi announces loudly for the room. The next hour flies by with oohs and aahs at little onesies, mama care kits, books, and other gifted odds and ends. Bella flies through the bags, handing me items with wild abandon.

As everyone leaves, my mom pulls me to the side of the room. "Where will you be delivering?"

"Why?" I ask, nerves coiling in my stomach.

"So that when you go to deliver, I can make sure to be there to support you." She says it like it's the most obvious thing in the world.

"With all due respect Mom, Tatum, and I will be the only ones present in the room when I give birth. After that, we'll have time where everyone can come and visit at home." I say sternly, trying to keep my cool.

"You don't want me there?" she throws back, impetuously. I swear she would be stomping her foot if she wasn't in a room full of people.

"That's not what I said."

"Will she be there?" She gestures across the room where Rose sits with Bella reading one of the books we received today.

"Rose? No, Mom, just like you, she will be coming and meeting her grandson after he is born and I've been able to rest." I stop, but then add, "But unlike you, she is okay with the choices that we've made regarding the birth of our child."

"Darcy Marie, that is no way to speak to your mother." She whisper yells, in an attempt to avoid drawing attention to us.

"Maybe if I felt respected, I would give it back. However, in the past seven months, instead of love and support from you, I've felt pushed to do the things that *you* want." My throat begins to clog and I quickly survey the room to make sure we don't have an audience. I catch Sin stealthily making her way across the room from the corner of my eye and her approach brings me a small sigh of relief.

"Ms. Whitestone, I think maybe it's time to go." Sin

interjects, her voice firm but not disrespectful. "Let me walk you out."

"I'll call you, Mom. Thank you for coming today." I manage to choke out, forcing a smile. Before I know what's come over me, I turn about and quickly make my way to Rose.

"Hey, sweetie." She smiles brightly at me but upon seeing the tears running down my face she changes her tone and says, "Oh Darcy, come here honey."

"Thank you. She's just so difficult." I sniffle into her shoulder.

"I know honey but I'm here for you when it's tough." Her love and empathy cocoon me just as tightly and warmly as her hug does. At this moment, I know that if I do want someone else in my delivery room, it will be her.

When Sin returns, she's got Harley in tow. She's pretty late considering she missed my entire baby shower. As much as I want to be upset with her, I know that she wouldn't want to miss this. I wish she would have at least let me know she wasn't going to make it on time.

"Darcy, I am so sorry." She sucks in a breath, eyes already overflowing with tears. "It was Benji, I... I... I'm done but he didn't make it easy for me to get out of there."

"Oh Harley, it's okay. We missed you though." I inspect her, looking for signs of mistreatment. "Are you okay? Did he hurt you?"

Fear flashes across her face but she shakes her head left to right quickly.

Chapter 23

Wake Up Call

Tatum ‖ 32 weeks pregnant, January

"Alright, so the little dude is measuring a bit bigger than we'd expect at this point. So he could come in two weeks, he could come in six or he could make us wait a little longer." Dr. Freyer tells us from her place beside the bed.

"So, what you are saying is we need to be prepared for his arrival because it could be anytime now?" I ask nervously, clenching and unclenching my fists that are concealed in my pockets.

"That is correct. You all will be parents soon!" Dr. Freyer claps excitedly.

"I, for one, am ready to give this little guy his eviction notice." Darcy chuckles, rubbing her stomach affectionately.

"You'll have an appointment at thirty-six weeks, and if you make it past that, then you'll have an appointment weekly. If we get to forty weeks and he still hasn't made his appearance, then we will start to talk about induction," says Dr. Freyer in closing.

"Sounds good, let's hope he makes the decision to move out on his terms." I smile at her, helping Darcy off the vinyl table and walking with her to the front desk, our hands intertwined to schedule our last few appointments.

AFTER OUR APPOINTMENT THURSDAY AFTERNOON, Darcy and I drove over to the beach bungalow for what she's calling our 'babymoon'. She explained it as a sort of honeymoon, but before the baby is born.

Laying in a lounge chair on the beach, her skin is bronzed from all the time she's been spending outside. Her breathing is slow and even. I know she needed this getaway weekend. The tension with her Mom at the baby shower cast a shadow on her mood and the last thing I want six weeks before the birth of our son, is for Darcy to be stressed. *So,* what better escape is there than her happy place?

Truthfully, the time away has been nice for me, too. Not only to relax and spend some time alone with Darcy, but one of the only places I feel like I can think clearly is here. Sitting with sand between my toes and the sun just hot enough to have me breaking a sweat, before I eventually dive into the waves and cool off.

"Want to go for a swim?" Darcy asks, squinting over at me, her sunkissed cheeks and brown eyes swirling with gold tones. They seem so much more vibrant under the glow of the sun.

"Yes, I was just thinking I was getting too warm." I

stand, dusting the sand from my legs, and go to help her out of the chair, keeping my fingers tangled in hers as we make our way into the water.

"Come here, Mama." I open my arms to her because she's standing too far away from me, and I want her close. She happily complies. I kiss her then turn her away from me so that I can hold her against me but as soon as her ass makes contact with my cock, he stands at attention. "Sorry."

"For what?" She chuckles, wiggling her ass against me knowing exactly what I'm apologizing for.

"Don't test me, I've been thinking about tearing this scrap of fabric you call a bathing suit off of you all day." I murmur in her ear, quiet enough that the families swimming ten feet away from us can't hear me, "I wouldn't hesitate to untie this and bury myself in you right now, if it weren't for the people around us. That, and the fact that you wouldn't be able to stay quiet for me."

"I think I'm ready for my afternoon delight." She feigns a yawn, leaning her head back against my shoulder and I grip her hip a little tighter, keeping her close to me.

"Haha, very funny. You and I both know that you need an afternoon nap, not an afternoon delight."

"You're right." She chuckles, pulling away from me and swiveling from side to side a bit.

"How are you feeling?"

"My back is killing me," she groans.

"Come here, lay back. The water should help alleviate some of the pressure, I'll keep you in place." She moves towards me, letting her body relax backwards into the water and I place my arms beneath her back, letting the water do a majority of the work.

"This is nice, how did you know it would help?" She

squints up at me, the sigh of relief that leaves her mouth is like music to my ears.

"Just been doing my research."

"Research." She continues to grill me with just a stare.

"Yes, the internet is a very informative place when you've never been a parent or with a pregnant woman before." I shrug, feigning nonchalance. She doesn't respond, instead letting her body relax.

Darcy yawns again a few moments later, bringing herself upright again. "I do think I need a nap, don't keep me waiting too long."

She brushes her lips lightly on mine before heading inside. I stay out in the water for a few more minutes, taking it all in; the sounds of the waves crashing into the sand, the birds chirping, and the children laughing help to soothe my racing heart. I haven't gotten used to her so openly sharing her affection with me, still struggling with feelings of inadequacy. Laying back, I let myself float with my thoughts until my limbs feel like noodles and I realize I have been wading in the water too long.

By the time I get inside, Darcy is already snoring softly in the bed. After quickly showering off any beachy remnants, I join her, letting myself drift off to sleep.

The next thing I know, I find myself groaning in pleasure, only to discover that there is warm, wet heat enveloping my cock. Thinking at first that I must be dreaming, when I find the strength to open my eyes and wake myself, I find that the warm, wet heat is very real and Darcy's mouth is swallowing my cock. Her brown eyes hooded with pleasure meet mine as she continues to bob up and down.

"You are so pretty like this." I manage, one hand caressing her cheek and then moving to the back of her head to guide her. She moans around my dick, coaxing extra warmth to build up my spine. "Baby, you have to stop, or I'm going to cum in your mouth."

She takes me to the back of her throat again before backing off for a breather "I wanted to make you feel good."

"But *I* want to make *you* feel good, Mama." I throw back at her, testing the waters to see what she's in the mood for. She lazily continues to stroke me as we speak. When Darcy joked about the abstinence phase, she wasn't joking. My hand and I have been getting along just fine in the meantime. When she does want me, I don't deny her but I have to admit that it's been a while, and fuck have I missed this.

"To be honest, I just want to do this for you. I'm not feeling very sexy right now," she confides while jerking me, sounding almost frustrated with herself.

"I think you look sexy as fuck, but I understand you've been uncomfortable recently."

"I have but your dick was poking me in the back after our nap and I wanted to touch you and that... Turned into this." Her cheeks pinken before she takes me into her mouth again, effectively ending the conversation. It isn't long before I'm shooting down her throat, she swallows every drop so beautifully.

"Your bath is ready, Mama, then how about a foot rub while we watch Gilmore Girls?" I ask, entering her room with her emotional support water bottle in one hand and a bowl of mixed berries, granola, and yogurt in the other.

Darcy still seemed beat after our little escapade earlier and I couldn't think of a better opportunity to relax than snacks and a bath. This also gives me time to cook her favorite dinner—lasagna, garlic bread, and salad, hold the onions.

"Oh, thank you! Help me in?" She smiles at me, lifting the comforter off. As she peels herself out of bed, she's still naked from earlier and I just can't give enough of her body this way. "Stop looking at me like that."

"Like what?" I wiggle my eyebrows at her before she rolls her eyes and I'm trailing her to the bathroom.

"Like you want to get me pregnant?"

"Already did that Mama and fully intend to do it again." I grin widely at her, setting her water and parfait next to her Kindle and phone on the tub caddy.

"Well, you can't... Not right now at least. Maybe in a few years."

"You mean I have to wait years to see you like this again?" I groan, approaching her from behind and making it a point to let her know what her body, vibrant with life, does to my dick.

"Tate." Pushing back into me, she moans, "Not tonight."

"I know baby, you need to relax. I just didn't want you to forget how fucking sexy you are." I spin her, planting a chaste kiss on her lips then holding her steady as she steps into the tub and leaving her to soak.

Chapter 24

Darcy Marie Whitestone, are you in fucking labor right now?

Darcy ‖ 38 weeks pregnant, February 19th

I probably shouldn't be attending this hockey game, considering that I could go into labor at literally any moment. I've felt kind of off all day, my back feeling tighter than normal, but I wasn't going to tell anyone only for them to make me stay home alone. It's the last qualifier to see if the guys move into the Stanley Cup, and it's been a tight season. I don't want to miss them securing their spot in another round, especially since Maverick rented a box for all of us. Logically, it wouldn't have been a big deal, but illogically I would rather be here with my friends and family.

I've secured a seat at the front of the box sitting with Victoria, Kodi's mom, while the girls stand in the back getting drinks before the game starts. Tatum is down in the tunnel with the guys just in case he has to handle anything, that hasn't stopped him from texting me several times to check-in.

TATUM

Are you sure you're feeling okay? You just didn't seem like yourself today, should we go to the hospital?

The answer to that question is probably yes, but until I'm having full-blown contractions, I'm not going in.

ME

I'm fine Tatum, if that changes, you will be the first to know. I love you.

TATUM

I better be, I love you too. I'll try to make it up there at some point.

ME

I'd love that, if not I'll see you after.

"He's worried about you isn't he?" Victoria asks, reading over my shoulder.

"Hey, nosey!" I lock my phone and place it in my lap, "but yes he is very worried."

"Well you are getting to that point, you probably shouldn't be here in all this excitement."

"I wasn't going to miss this game. It might be the last one of the season."

"Okay, whatever you say sweetie." She smiles softly at me, I know she wants to mom me but I think she can tell that I'm not feeling that right now.

The lights in the arena dim, and the girls, plus Bella, join us at the front of the box, screaming, hooting, and hollering for the guys as they skate onto the ice. Maverick of course finds the box, pointing his stick at his girls,and placing his hand over his heart. I wonder if Tate would've done something similar for me had he been able to continue playing after his injury.

The puck drops and all hell breaks loose, the Houston Knights manage to get possession of the puck and beeline it for Nik and the net. Dom isn't about to let that happen but when one of the opposing players bumps him, he loses his mind. Out of the corner of my eye, I see Sin's hands cover her mouth as she watches Dom grab him by the jersey and push him back. They both end up in the penalty box leaving Nik with one less person helping protect the net and letting Houston secure the first goal of the game.

It's the final period of the game, and I'm standing with my hands on my lower back. As the game has progressed, so has my back pain. During the second period, I began to feel an occasional tightening in my abdomen. They were pretty far apart at first, but now we are in the final period and they are getting closer together. My chest is heaving with each one. When I see Kodi nudge Sin out of the corner of my eye, I know I'm done for.

"Darcy Marie Whitestone, are you in fucking labor right now?" Sinclair yells, visibly pissed I didn't say anything.

"Uh, no? I mean... I don't know. Yes?" I smile sheepishly at her.

"Oh my god." Harley rolls her eyes, "I'm calling Tate. Let's go."

In a flash, Bella is in Victoria's arms, and Kodi is guiding me out of the box and down to the player exit. Sin is leading the charge, and everyone else follows closely behind us as Harley speaks quietly into the phone. Tatum's Porsche squeals to a halt in front of the door and he jumps out, breathing heavily as he approaches me.

"Darcy, Mama, are you okay? What can I do?" Tatum's voice is filled with tension as he flings the door to the Porsche open for me, helping me in and securing my seatbelt.

"Getting me to the hospital would be a great place to start." I grit as another contraction hits.

"See you all there!" He yells before hopping in, leaving our friends in the dust.

"Did you call Rose?"

"As soon as I hung up with Harley."

"We need to call Dr. Freyer and I'll text my mom," I tell him, trying to keep my breathing even and dialing the number they gave for when labor starts.

"Tampa Hospital, this is Leanne, how can I help you?" A high-pitched yet bubbly voice greets through the phone.

"I'm in labor." That's all I can get out before a gush of liquid leaves my body, "holy shit my water broke."

"Oh fuck." Tatum's tone is calm, but the way his shoulders bunch and the car starts moving a little faster betrays him.

"Okay, ma'am, are you on your way in? What's your name and who is your doctor? How far apart are your contractions?" Leanne quizzes calmly, keys clacking in the background.

"We should be there in the next ten minutes. My name is Darcy Whitestone and it's Dr. Freyer. Contractions are about four minutes apart right now."

"Okay Ms. Whitestone, you'll pull up outside the labor and delivery ER entrance and then we will get you all settled in," she instructs.

"Thank you, see you soon." I hang up the phone,

leaning my head back and breathing through the contraction. "I'm sorry."

"For what?"

"Not telling you sooner that I was having contractions."

"It's okay, honestly I could tell something was off but I didn't want to force you to leave until you were ready." He grins, pulling the car in front of the ER. An orderly is waiting with a wheelchair and assists me out of the car. "I have to go park the car, I'll see you in there."

"Wait, I don't want you to leave." My throat clogs, fear setting in now that we've arrived.

"Mama, I can't-"

"I've got it." Kodi's voice comes from behind Tate, "Get her inside and I'll get the cars switched out."

"Thank you." We say in unison before Tatum tosses Ko the keys and pushes me inside and to reception.

The next few minutes are a flurry of questions and me breathing through the pain, getting wristbands and then we are being wheeled up to the labor and delivery floor by Trina, the nurse who will be with us until shift change.

"Ready for this, Mama?" Tatum asks in that horrific, familiar accent and, because of the pain and the onslaught of another contraction, the faux accent irrationally pisses me off. He's trying to break the tension but now that I'm here and faced with pushing a whole ass child out of my vag, I'm not having it.

"Now is not the fucking time, Tatum Reed. I will kill you." I seethe, screaming as another, larger contraction strikes. Trina laughs under her breath. I'm sure this isn't the first time she's heard this and I can guarantee it won't be the last.

THE EPIDURAL WAS A MAGNIFICENT INVENTION. The contractions are muted but I have been in labor for eight hours at this point and I'm only dilated four centimeters. Kodi switched out the Porsche for my car since that's where the carseat is installed, Tatum had Mav double-check no less than three times that it was properly installed. Along with grabbing our go bags and dropped them off while our friends have taken up residence in the waiting room. The guys lost their game and then when they saw their texts, got here as fast as they could.

"Do you need anything?" Tate asks, leg bouncing as he sits beside the bed, hand in mine.

"No, but I think if everyone is still sitting out in the waiting room. They should go home and get some rest. We can call when he comes." I tell him, rubbing my stomach, "Plus you probably need a walk and some coffee. You haven't left my side since we got here and, though I appreciate it, you need to take care of yourself too."

"You're probably right. I won't be gone too long but if anything happens, call me please."

"I'll be okay Tate." He places his forehead on mine, kissing me softly before he exits the room. I find myself relaxing in the quiet of the room, letting my eyes drift close for a moment.

Chapter 25

It's Time

Tatum || 38 weeks pregnant, February 19th

I wave to the nurses as they open the doors into the hallway for me and I cross the hall into the room. My parents, the twins, Bella, and our best friends are sprawled across the small waiting area. Dom's head rests on Nik's shoulder as he reads a book, Harley and Sin scroll their phones, Bella colors with Tessa and Tinsley, Victoria and Dale sit in the corner with my parents speaking quietly while Maverick holds Kodi close. All eyes come up to me as I enter the area.

"Is she okay?" Kodi's eyes are red rimmed, as if she's been crying. I'm sure that she's worried about her best friend.

"Is he here?" My mom asks.

"Baby!" Bella squeals, clapping her hands.

"I heard baby!" Dom's eyes pop open as he finds me across the room.

"How are you doing? Do you need anything?" Mavericks asks.

"She's okay. I'm okay. He's not here and he honestly won't be for a while. You all should go home, shower, rest and I'll call when he's here." I tell them, exhaustion weighing heavily in my bones.

"My daughter is here, Darcy Whitestone. She's in labor, she needs me." I hear echoing from the hallway. Everyone we want here is in this room. Lorraine Whitestone had the audacity to show up to the hospital after Darcy told her she could visit after he was born. I'm turning and exiting the room with Collins, Nik and Sinclair hot on my heels.

"She actually isn't having anyone in the room except for her partner, ma'am," Wesley, the nurse on desk duty, tells the Whitestones. Steven stands beside his wife, arms crossed over his chest.

"That's impossible, I'm her Mother you have to let me in." Lorraine demands.

"Oh Lorraine, it is so lovely to see you!" Sinclair says, her voice laced with saccharine sweetness. Lorraine and Steven turn to us and while Steven's expression remains neutral, Lorraine plasters on a fake smile.

"Tatum, sweetheart! Tell the nice man that I need a wristband to go see Darcy." She walks towards me, arms wide open. Wanting to avoid causing a scene, I let her wrap her arms around me.

"You know I can't do that, Lorainne. Darcy and I will be in the delivery room and then we will be doing visits in waves, but I do remember her saying you both would be welcome to visit us at *home*," I tell her.

"Why is everyone else here then?" Steven's gruff voice interrupts.

"We were all getting ready to head out. We were together when she went into labor, wanted to make sure they were settled and Tatum had caffeine before we left," Nik responds, voice just as gruff.

"I don't remember asking you." Steven spits.

"And I don't remember Darcy or Tatum asking you to be here." Sin keeps her sweet smile in place.

"Mr. Reed, do I need to call security?" Wesley asks from behind the desk.

"I don't know, does he, Lorraine?" I quirk a brow at her.

"No, no you don't. We will just walk with everyone else out." She smiles at me then Wesley.

"I will call you once he comes, and yes, we will send pictures. I know you're excited," I assuage because as much as she aggravates me, I won't cause a scene with her parents in the middle of this waiting room. The last thing Darcy needs right now is more stress. Her comfort is my top priority right now. I give Steven a curt nod before saying goodbye to my friends, grabbing a coffee, and heading back into the room with Darcy.

THIS WOMAN IS A WARRIOR, she's been in labor for over forty hours. Nurses have been coming and going, manually checking her dilation. We've finally gotten to the point that she can deliver our son vaginally. There was a brief window where Dr. Freyer wanted to consider a c-section, but the little guy decided he was ready to stop tormenting his Mom. Darcy has breathed through every contraction like a champ. I've been steadily delivering ice chips and giving her small words of encouragement when she lets me near enough— any semblance of personal space has ebbed and flowed, considering how frequently it has been invaded since our arrival at the hospital.

"Okay, Darcy, are we ready to push this little guy out?" Dr. Freyer enters the room, washing up and getting herself into position to help us deliver. A few others enter as well, get Darcy in position to push, and wheel in a neonatal warmer. We got lucky that by coincidence she was already on the premises when we arrived. She's been here the whole time.

"God, I would love to get him out." She moans, her forehead is licked with sweat, her hair is disheveled, and deep purple bags reside beneath her eyes.

"Tatum, you're going to hold one leg and Nurse May is going to hold the other. Talk her through it, encourage her, count with her. Darcy, the next contraction you get, push for ten seconds and then release. We will do that until he comes." I position myself accordingly with Dr. Freyer's instructions and we wait for the next contraction to hit. When it does, Darcy braces herself and begins pushing. She cries out in anguish, and it hurts me to see her feeling this way.

"You've got this, Darcy, baby." I tell her when she relaxes back into the bed.

"Looks like another one is coming." Nurse May says, "You're going to have to go again, Darcy."

We repeat this cycle a few more times, Darcy is growing tired. I can see it in her eyes. She cussed out the room a few times, cried that she couldn't do this but still managed to pull herself back together and brace herself to push again. And again. And again.

"He's crowning, Tatum can you see?" Dr. Freyer asks, I look down to see the top of a head filled with blonde hair peeking out of Darcy. "Darcy, we've got maybe two more and then your little boy will be in your arms."

"You're doing so well Mama. I'm so proud of you. He's almost here." I smile at her, brushing the hair from her face, and she smiles weakly back.

After one more contraction and a long push to get his body out completely, tiny wails fill the room, and our son is placed on Darcy's bare chest. I continue to support Darcy's leg, as they clean her up but lean in to kiss her, whispering and telling her how proud of her I am for what she's done. We both look at our son and my heart is filled with so much love that it could burst. They take him to clean him up before wrapping him in a tiny burrito blanket and handing him to me. I sit beside the woman I love with our son in my arms and he looks at me like he knows who I am, that I made him and what I think is a smile spreads across his small, chubby face. Who knew that such a tiny soul could change my whole world?

Chapter 26

Heissoprecious!

Darcy ‖ 1 day old, February

The first twenty-four hours with our son fly by in a flurry of cries—from all parties—dirty diapers and breastfeeding. It feels like a full-time job but, no job has ever felt so dearly rewarding at the same time. Tatum has been by my side through it all, helping whenever and however he can, even letting me rest in between feeds. I've heard him telling our son about the people he will be meeting today, starting with Rose, Walter, and the twins.

A soft knock sounds on the door, followed by Rose peeking her head in, a wide grin spreading across her face when she sees Tatum, baby and I sitting in the bed together.

"Hi, my dears." She approaches the bed, placing a gentle hand on my shoulder then rounding the bed and pulling Tatum into a hug before looking down at her grandson and immediately bursting into tears, "he's beautiful."

"Thanks, Mom. Darcy was a champ and they are both doing so well. If everyone wants to wash their hands, you guys can hold him. He just ate and pooped and he gives the best cuddles so he should be good for a bit, right Mama?" Tatum says before seeking a nod of approval from me, which I give. Tessa and Tinsley eagerly cross the room to the sink, my parents following closely behind them.

"Walter, why don't you hold him first?" I ask, having already run this by Rose. She's eager to hold her grandson but this feels like a big moment and she understands that.

"I'd love that." Walter smiles and the twins grumble about having to wait to hold their first nephew ever which causes Tatum to chuckle as I hand off our son.

Walter gets comfortable on the blue vinyl couch that's doubled as Tatum's bed before creating a crook in his elbow where Tatum places the baby. Walter takes a moment to take him in before asking, "So what name did you land on?"

"Tell him, babe." Tatum directs toward me as he hovers over his dad.

"We'd like for you all to meet Hayden..." I pause smiling towards Tatum's father, "Walter Reed."

"You didn't!" He says a little louder than intended, waking Hayden. Fortunately, after a brief whine and wriggle in Grandpa's arms, he calms back to sleep almost immediately. Tears stream down Walters face as he passes Hayden to Rose, immediately pulling his son into a hug, "That means so much to me. More than you could ever know."

"We felt like he needed a strong middle name from a strong male figure in his life." I say through my own tears.

"Oh guys, that is so wonderful." Rose's voice is filled with so much glee.

"Not to break up the cry fest but can I hold my nephew now?" Tessa says with a little too much attitude.

"Watch it." That's all Walter has to say for Tessa to

pantomime zipping her lips closed and tossing the key to Tinsley, who basketball shoots it over to the trash can in the corner.

"You guys are ridiculous." I laugh.

The Reeds spend the next hour with us, passing Hayden around under Tate's watchful eyes, and chatting before they head out. We get a ten minute break before another knock sounds and our best friends enter the room.

"Oh my goodness!" Kodi cries as she rushes towards the bed where I sit with Hayden wrapped in a little burrito close to my chest. She slows before sitting gently and wrapping her arms around my neck, "Are you okay? I know it's been uneventful so far, but I was so worried."

"Ko, breathe. I'm great and your nephew is so excited to meet you."

When I say that, her eyes grow big and her arms maternally form that safe little spot in her elbow for me to place Hayden. Sin and Harley approach from behind her, taking in Hayden's small form, watery eyes and soft smiles adorn their faces.

"*Heissoprecious!*" From behind Sin, Dom's sentence comes out as one giant word, muddied by his excitement. Nik and Collins approach the other side of the bed and I'm suddenly feeling a little claustrophobic. I meet Tatum's eye and he wordlessly understands my escalating panic.

"Hey guys, why don't we back up a little bit? I think D has had a lot of people in her personal space and might not want so many people in her bubble. Kodi, wanna come sit over here?" Tatum gestures to the chair in the corner of the room and everyone slowly dissipates from around me, allowing me to suck in a deep, cleansing breath.

Our friends stay until visiting hours are finished, taking turns with Hayden. Nik even catered food for us to have family dinner together. Stu brought Bella by briefly, her small giggles causing a domino effect when Hayden smiled at her from Maverick's lap. I can see their friendship blossoming already and I can tell that they are going to be thick as thieves—just like their Mamas.

THIS MORNING we've received the all-clear to head home from the hospital, and now Tatum is triple-checking the car seat in my car. He drives us home at exactly the speed limit —no more, no less. Hayden's uninterrupted slumber next to me has helped to ease some of Tatum's anxiety. It's cute how protective and careful he is, but fuck am I ready to be home and to sleep in my bed. Or rather Tatum's.

"I'll get him out, if you want to grab the duffle," Tatum whispers as he puts my car into park and jumps out to open my door for me, helping me carefully out of the car. He's been so ginger in his touches, scared he might break me because my body is still hurting and healing.

"Thanks, Daddy." I slip him a sly grin as I follow him in.

"You can't say things like that for at least..." He pauses looking at his watch, "the next forty days."

"I can't help it, that's your new title."

"Fine." He sighs, as he unclicks the carseat and we head into the elevator. Hayden begins to stir a bit and looking at my phone, I realize how close it is to feeding time.

"We have fifteenish minutes to give him the grand tour of our condo. Then, he has to eat. I was thinking we could do a bath and bedtime together. I feed, you read?"

"That sounds nice," he asserts, pulling me into his side. His lips caress the top of my head, keeping me there until the doors ding at the condo and I have to swipe us in.

"This is the entryway, your Mama requires everyone to take their shoes off so don't forget to do that." I find myself rolling my eyes as I routinely slip my shoes off and we continue deeper into the condo.

"The living room is to your right, we will introduce you to Gilmore Girls when you're probably ten or eleven. To the left is the kitchen and dining room. We will eat *lots* of lasagna here."

"I am who I am, a woman who loves lasagna, very easy to please." I chuckle because we do eat more lasagna than the average household.

"Let's show you to your bedroom. Your Mama, Daddy, Aunts, and Uncles worked hard on making this space unique and special for you little man," Tatum coos, setting the car seat down and squatting to pull Hayden out. There's something about the man you love, holding the child you created together that just brings your ovaries to life. "Come here, Mama."

I join Tatum and Hayden in the middle of the room, as Tatum quietly shows Hayden all the tiny details that we put into bringing this room to life—taking extra care to point out the little touches I was responsible for including.

"Welcome home, little guy." I say quietly, placing a kiss on his forehead before placing one on Tatum's lips.

Chapter 27

Hold me?

Tatum ‖ 2 weeks old, February

"Come on buddy, Mama is trying to rest," I tell my crying son, his little face scrunched in anger, cheeks aflame from his screaming. I fed him pumped breastmilk, read him Goodnight Moon, walked in circles around his room, and rocked him for over thirty minutes and yet he still won't relax. Right when I think that he's calming, the vicious cycle starts all over again. My patience has long since run out.

"Hey, I can take over. Go rest," implores a groggy Darcy from the entryway of Hayden's room, offering me a soft smile. Her hair is tied in a messy bun, and my t-shirt hangs off her shoulder. Despite Darcy being a trooper and our son being everything we wished for---I don't feel like Darcy and I have gotten a wink of sleep over the past two weeks. She's powering through, and being a wonderful Mom but I can't say the same about being a Dad. I feel like no matter what I do, I'm doing it wrong. That no matter how hard I try, I can't win with my son.

"Baby, you need to sleep. You were up with him all night." I try continuing to sway from side to side with our son in my arms who squirms in my hold. His neck craning in Darcy's direction.

"I know Tate, but I can't sleep when I can hear him wailing across the condo. Just let me get him down and then I can sleep too." She sighs, sounding frustrated and I can't blame her. We've been home for two weeks and I feel useless. Every time I pick Hayden up, he starts crying. Darcy keeps saying it's because she spends so much time feeding him and he lived inside of her, but I can't help but think that he hates me. When Darcy has to take him out of my hands, I feel like she is going to resent me because then when does she get to rest? I can't even let her rest right.

"Come on, hand him over. I'll be in soon." She comes closer, opening her arms for Hayden. As soon as he is in her arms, he relaxes and my heart cinches in pain again thinking that he really does hate me.

"I'm sorry."

That's all I say, I don't have the capacity to stand there as she lulls Hayden to sleep. I don't have the right words to tell her how angry I am at myself for not being able to help more or to tell her that I'm so scared I'm not enough of a partner in this. I do my best. Even with Hayden resisting me, I'm cleaning, cooking, and making sure Darcy is taking care of herself, but it doesn't feel like enough. *I don't feel like enough.*

I pace back and forth in the kitchen, two mugs of chamomile tea steeping, ready and waiting for Darcy to exit Hayden's room. Three anxious minutes later, his door clicks open and closed, and she makes her way into the kitchen. How the hell does she get him down so quickly?

"You should be sleeping." She says, her facial expression solemn.

"So should you. I made tea. I'm hoping it will help us relax and get a little sleep before he wakes up." We both sip our teas in the deafening silence of our kitchen.

"Hold me?" She asks, a desperation in her voice. I know she can feel the disconnect between us since we've brought Hayden home. Her focus has been solely on making sure he is eating, sleeping and breathing. We haven't had any true alone time because on the rare occasion that we can rest, we do.

"I'd love to." We make the trek to our room, setting our mugs down and sliding into bed. I open my arms for Darcy and she slides in so effortlessly, tucking her head under my chin and placing her leg over mine.

"You're doing so good, Tatum. He's just a baby and he's getting used to the world. *Please* don't fade out on me. I need you and so does he, even if you don't see it yet." She whispers into the dark room.

I blow out a breath, stroking her back gently, "I'm trying not to Mama. I love you both so much."

"I know and that's why I'm telling you we need you. You are enough, you're doing enough."

"Thank you." I grip her jaw, guiding her mouth to mine gently, "let's try and rest."

Darcy sinks further into my arms, her eyes closing and we are both out within minutes. We are no sooner jolted awake by tiny cries coming from Darcy's phone and it takes us a moment to come back to planet earth. Darcy slowly begins to roll out of bed, "he needs to eat. I'll bring him back in here so he can be with us both."

"You stay, I'll go grab him." I say, grabbing her wrist gently to keep her from going any further.

"Maybe change his diaper before you come in."

"Yes, Mama, be right back." I quickly head towards Hayden's room, changing his diaper then placing him into Darcy's arms. I sit with Darcy in silence as she feeds Hayden, once he's fed she hands him over to me and he sleeps peacefully in my arms for an hour while Darcy and I stare at an episode of Gilmore Girls. The way he nuzzles into my arm makes me feel at peace, even if it's just for a moment.

ANOTHER NIGHT PASSES by where Darcy has to be awake with Hayden because my presence isn't enough for him, I can feel my anxious energy running rampant and I feel like I need to get out of the house for a minute before I lose my mind.

"Mind if I run to the gym for an hour?" I ask Darcy, already changing my outfit as she gets Hayden settled against her breast. A quick flash of disappointment, or maybe fear goes over her face before she replaces it with a small smile.

"Yeah, we will probably be here a minute anyway. Want to grab soup and salad from that new place on your way back for lunch?" She asks with a tinge of uncertainty in her voice.

"Of course, text me what you want and I'll pick it up on my way back." I pepper gentle kisses on both her and Hayden's foreheads, before making my protein shake and heading down to the Porsche. I throw my workout bag into the passenger seat before sliding into the driver's side.

"Get it together, dude. She even told you that you're doing great and they need you." I say out loud to no one but myself but that doesn't seem enough to calm my energy. Pressing the ignition and backing the car out of my parking space, I find myself turning right heading the opposite way of the gym. *A drive, a drive will clear my mind.*

The name Dominic Montez pops up on my screen so I press the little green phone button, "Hey Dom."

"What's up, dude? How are y'all doing?" His voice breaks through the car speakers.

"Hayden is not sleeping well man, it's kind of wild." I try to laugh it off but even I can hear the strain in my voice, barely keeping it together.

"Why don't you guys have your Mom come help a little bit?"

"She's got a cold right now, and can't make it over for a few days, otherwise she'd be here already."

"Damn dude, that blows. If Coach wasn't railing us into the ice for losing our qualifier, I would be offering to come over more." Would Hayden cry in the arms of mine or Darcy's closest friends, or is it just me?

"I know man, thanks for checking in."

"Are... Are you sure you're good, man? Feels like you've been kind of spacey since he was born."

"That's what happens when a kid enters the picture, man. Listen, I'm pulling into the gym, call you later," I lie.

"Yep... Okay bye, good luck!" Dom hangs up the phone and I realize that in the moments that I was talking to Dom, I've pulled onto the interstate and am heading West. To what destination? I don't know. It's unlike me to lie to my friends.

Chapter 28

Six hours

Darcy || 2 weeks old, February

Six hours. That's how long Tatum has been gone, I've called everyone and no one has seen him. I called the gym, he never checked in. After calling his parents, the arena, and every hospital within a fifty mile radius, I've come to the conclusion that he's given up on us.

"Come on, Tatum. Answer the fucking phone." It rings and rings again, for probably the twentieth time before going to voicemail. He turned his find my friends off and he won't answer any of our calls or texts.

"D? Where are you?" Kodi comes around the corner of our living room, finding me in a pile of tissues, Hayden sleeping soundly in his baby tot beside me. I see her and my dam breaks, sobs wracking my body uncontrollably.

"Why..." I can't catch my breath, gulping for air, "why would he do this to me? Why." Another gulp for air, "wouldn't he just talk to me?"

Kodi's arms wrap around me and she speaks quietly, yet firmly, "Breathe for me, D."

"In." *One. Two. Three.* "Out." *One. Two. Three.* We repeat the cycle two more times before I feel ready enough to have a conversation.

"I don't know what he's thinking but I'm sure he will be back, okay? He never checked in at the gym?" She asks.

"Nope. Hasn't called anyone and isn't answering either. Dom said he spoke to him briefly and he sounded jumpy, but didn't give him any information to lead him to believe he was going to bolt."

"I can't get a hold of Harls but Sin is heading over with an overnight bag." It's then that I notice she dropped one in the living room as well. "We will stay as long as you need us."

"What about Bella?" I ask, knowing that she has a child to take care of too.

"Stu is going to help while Mav is at practice and then she will come stay with us Friday if that's okay."

"Yeah, I could use some Bella snuggles for sure."

"I'm here!" Sin gasps for air as she enters the condo, "Sorry it took so long. What can I do? Oh my god, this place is disgusting. I'm cleaning." While I should be offended at her bluntness, it doesn't surprise me and she's not wrong, in the six hours that Tatum has been gone, it looks like a tornado came through here.

"Thank you guys," I say through sniffles, looking at my son and hoping for his sake that his Dad gets his shit together soon.

"When does Hayden need to eat next?" Kodi's lilting voice breaks through my brain fog.

"Probably an hour or so."

"When did you shower last?"

"The other night, it's been rough. We've been trying our

best, he was doing his best." I say again as another sob escapes me.

"Why don't you go shower and take a nap? You need it and he will be okay with me. You have bottles in the fridge right? I know how to heat them."

"That would be really great actually thank you. He's been gassy though so he needs to be fed at that weird angle and just keep him upright for a bit."

"We've got you both Darcy. Go, love you."

"Love you," Sin says from behind the couch where she's collecting tissues, chocolate wrappers, and diapers.

"Love you both."

I head to our room, turning on the shower at the highest temperature. Once the bathroom is filled with steam, I strip and step under the water, just letting it run over my body as the adrenaline from the past few hours wears off and the exhaustion kicks in. Throughout my shower, salty tears stream down my face, my body shaking with each sob that leaves my throat. When I've cried all the tears I have left, I step out of the shower, grab one of Tatum's shirts, and pull the covers of our bed up to my neck. Before I let my eyes close, I pull my phone out and send one final message to him. If he doesn't answer this one then I'm going to give up.

ME

Tatum, please. Please don't do this to us. We need you, you didn't even tell me you were leaving. You left me, our son without a word. Why? Why did you do this? We love you and want you to come home.

Now I sit here with his parents and sisters, a week later, wondering what went so horribly wrong that he would just disappear on us like this. My three-week-old son and I that he claimed to want and love.

"This doesn't make sense. He's never been one to just run off like this," Rose sighs. Tessa and Tinsley sit in the corner of the couch with Hayden between them since they couldn't make up their minds about who should get to hold him first.

"All he said was that he was headed to the gym. I figured he needed to get away for a bit, we had a few rough nights with Hayden." I shrug, my legs tucked beneath me, one of our fuzzy blankets covering my body and providing me some semblance of comfort. Not the kind that I wish I was experiencing and comes in the form of Tatum's arms wrapped tightly around me.

"There's not anywhere that you can think of that he might have run off to?" Walter asks for the third time since they arrived two hours ago.

"I don't think so."

"No place of peace or comfort that he likes to escape to?" He expands on his previous question. An epiphany punches me in the face right then of the one place that he always says he goes to when he needs to think. A place that we've escaped to multiple times over the last nine and half months when life got to be too overwhelming or pregnancy got to be too hard.

"Oh my god. The beach house!" I scream, scaring Hayden into tears. Tinsley quickly scoops him up, softly hushing him back to sleep before leaning back and letting him sleep on her chest. Tessa side eyes her, probably assuming that it's going to be a while before she gets some nephew snugs.

Rose and Walter are up on their feet as soon as the words leave my mouth, slipping on their shoes and quickly telling the twins, "Behave, help Darcy, and share your nephew's snuggles or Darcy has the right to step in." In an instant they are rushing out of the condo.

I silently will Tatum to be at the bungalow and pray his parents will be able to knock some sense into him. I know that if he does come back, he has a lot of making up to do. I refuse to just go back to normal and act like he didn't crack my heart in two when he walked out on me and his son.

Chapter 29

You think?

Tatum ‖ 3 weeks old, February

The front door of the beach house slams open and I'm swiftly slapped on the back of the head by, as it turns out, none other than my mother. I've seen my parents angry, and I've been scolded and grounded more times than I can count, but the pure rage radiating off of my mom tells me all that I need to know. I fucked up, and I fucked up bad. It hasn't left my mind since I drove away last week but it's time to face the music.

"Tatum Michael Reed, are you even listening to me right now?" My mother snaps her fingers in my face far more aggressively than necessary. I honestly don't remember how long she was rampaging or anything that she said to me.

"Rose honey, I know this is going to put me in the dog house but why don't you take a breather and we sit down and talk to him." My dad says as he gently guides her to the loveseat across from where I sit.

"I'm sorry." I don't know what else to say at this point but it's worth a shot.

"What were you thinking, son?" My dad asks, I catch him rubbing soothing circles on my Mom's shoulder and wonder who's been doing that for Darcy over this past week.

"I..." I choke on my words, emotions I haven't wanted to face getting stuck at the base of my throat. "I am the worst dad to ever exist. Hayden cries every time he's in my arms, Darcy resents me, and I'll never be as good as you." I let the tears stream freely down my face, not bothering to hide my hatred for myself from my parents.

"Is that what you think?" My mom asks, tears pooling in her own eyes.

"I don't simply think it, the past three weeks have proven it."

"Your actions and words according to Darcy paint a different picture," Dad adds in.

"You don't think I replay her words over and over in my head?" I cry out, my breaths coming in heavier. "You think that I didn't hear all of the praise she gave me? I know she thinks I'm enough! She doesn't understand that it's not about what she thinks of me, it's that I don't feel like enough!" I poke myself in the chest, screwing my eyes shut and trying to ward off the cracks that continue to break inside my chest.

"You won't know that you aren't good enough if you quit before you've had the chance to get started." My mom's voice is now beside me and her hand comes to my back, gently circling like she would do when I would get upset when I was younger. I find myself leaning into her touch, seeking out the comfort.

"How do I fix it? She's got to hate me by now." I can't

live without her, I love her and will do anything to get her back, but those words are reserved for her alone.

"You get in your car, you go home and you communicate. You work for it. She's worried sick over this, Son. All she wants is for you to be back with them and for you to talk to her. She might *need* more after that and you best believe you're going to have to put in the work for it." Dad speaks softly, "Do you remember when your sisters were born, and Aunt Bea came and stayed over for a few weeks? That was because we brought your sisters home and all they did was cry, your mom cried, and I cried. We didn't know what to do, but we knew that if we stayed on the path we were on, it was going to negatively impact our marriage and you three. So we had a conversation, we figured it out and we fought damn hard. We even went to therapy a few times while you were in school. Healing a relationship is a slow and painful process. My point is this, if you truly love something or someone, you will fight until every emotional bone in your body is bruised, battered, and broken."

"Oh." My mind swirls as I try to process this tidal wave of information, things I didn't realize my parents faced because they sheltered us from them all the while. "What if she can't forgive me?"

"While I don't see that happening, if it does, you two will figure out how to proceed," Mom says softly.

"Well, it appears I have my work cut out for me. I'm sorry that I worried you all."

"It's okay, Son, let's go." At that, we are grabbing my gym bag and loading into our cars.

PULLING into my parking spot at the condo has my stomach tied in knots. My parents were following closely behind me as we drove back over the bridge into Tampa. I step out of the car, nodding to my parents where they wait for the twins to come downstairs. Stepping into the elevator, the floors tick by, and with each ding, my anxiety ratchets up a notch, my stomach clenches and my heart races until the doors slide open and I step into the condo. My sisters pass me in the hallways, giving me small yet sympathetic smiles.

My steps slow as I get closer to the living space and when I round the corner, I'm greeted by Darcy's puffy, red eyes—tears rolling down her face and onto the blanket that Hayden is wrapped in. My feet quickly take me across the room but I stop in my tracks when she flinches the slightest bit, afraid of my touch. My fragile facade crumbles instantly, because what kind of man am I to cause this much damage? I opt to sit beside her on the couch, giving her a foot of space between us.

"I'm sorry, Mama." I say through my tears, "I am so fucking sorry."

"Please don't call me that right now." Her voice is cold and detached.

"Can I hold him while we talk?" She doesn't say anything, but hands me our son then shuts me out by scooting to the corner of the couch and pulling her legs into her chest. For the first time, our son doesn't wriggle or scream in my arms. He just looks at me, confusion etched into his tiny features and the fissures in my heart widen even more. My son's calm, as meaningful as it is, is overshadowed by the rest of this little life we created for him shattering around me.

"Go ahead, Tatum, because I don't know what to say to you right now."

"I shouldn't have left like that."

"You think?" She laughs, dejectedly.

"I wasn't thinking clearly. I should have stayed and talked to you. I know that's all I needed to do and now I've done irreparable damage to our relationship."

"It's not irreparable but I'm not ready to take you back." With that statement from her, the fissures crack even more, my heart soon to be in pieces on the floor—it will all be my fault.

"That's warranted, I fucked up. I needed time to think but instead of coming back to you both, I ran. I can't even tell you why I did it. I was planning on heading to the gym but then I turned in the opposite direction and I hate myself for that."

"Then why did you do it, Tate?" Her body visibly shakes as she weeps beside me and all I want to do is scoop her into my arms and soothe her but I know that's the opposite of what she needs from me right now.

"No matter how many times you thanked me, told me I was doing enough, that you loved me, the fear that you were starting to resent me for not being helpful with him grew to monstrous levels."

"Do you really believe that I resent you?" She asks the question and I can hear her voice softening the more we speak but her body language remains closed off.

"No. In fact, I know that every word you spoke to me was said with sincerity and love behind it but every perceived failure came with a whisper, echoing how it was only a matter of time before you changed your mind." I'm laying my cards out at my feet, being honest and it's terrifying.

"Because we built trust and love and growth here, Tate. And you threw it all away because you were what? Scared?"

She throws her arms in the air, the bitterness seeping through her tone. "I was fucking scared too! You disappeared! I didn't even know if you were alive or if I was going to have to raise our son alone! I was worried sick, like made myself vomit over this, my milk supply dropped, and I've had panic attacks almost every day."

I feel my head drop between my shoulders, tears still falling from both of our eyes, my body vibrating with anger towards myself.

"I'm so fucking sorry, Darcy. You're right. I shouldn't have left like that and I swear I won't do it again." I need to face the consequences of my actions and I need to prove to Darcy that I won't do that stupid shit again.

"I think you should stay with your parents, you can come to see him whenever you want but I need space. I can't share a bed with you, have conversations with you, or work on building a life with you right now."

Her words are frantic yet firm. I hold Hayden close to my chest, whispering soft affection to him before handing him to Darcy and packing a duffle of my things.

Heading out, I promise, "No matter what, I'm going to fight. Fight for you and Hayden. For our family. I love you."

"Goodbye, Tate." Her sniffles echo, following me down the hallway and into the elevator.

Chapter 30

My Heart on the Kitchen Floor

Darcy ‖ 4 weeks old, March

True to his word, every day since Tatum showed back up at the condo and apologized, he's been making time to see Hayden. I want to think that he's coming to see me, but I refuse to let myself believe it. His week-long vanishing act lingers in the back of my head and the idea he might do it again when things get hard roils within me.

When he arrives, he's never empty handed. Some days he comes with lilies, and he's brought lasagna—he even asked if we could eat together but I wasn't ready. I can't sit across from him and have a conversation, when my heart has hardly even healed from last week.

I've been using Rose as a way to get me out of talking to him. She's been helping me with Hayden and holding me when I cry, she validates my fear and anger towards her son. While I know that deep down she wants to shake us both and tell us not to throw this all away. On the other side of the coin, my mother won't leave me alone. She calls everyday and when I don't pick up, she calls three more times. I know she's fine because she texts afterward, but I can't deal with her on top of this.

Today, though, it's just me and Hayden, so when the elevator dings open I take a deep breath and steel myself to face Tate unassisted. Hayden sleeps quietly in his crib so I turn from the kitchen counter to find Tate standing there and looking at me with trepidation in his eyes, a box of diapers in hand.

"Hi. I brought more diapers, I noticed they were getting low." He sets them on the island and waits.

"Thank you."

"Could we talk before he gets up?"

"I was actually going to shower before he wakes up if you want to watch him on the monitor app." I still don't feel ready to have this conversation, the one where he sits in front of me and tells me all the things I believe and know in an effort to bring us back together.

"Ma-" He stops himself, "Darcy please."

"I... I can't Tatum." I turn on my heel to head down the hallway but before I can breach the entranceway, he's in front of me. His desperate, hazel eyes shout a million truths that I don't want to hear right now. I squeeze my eyes shut, warding off the tears and eye contact threatening to break me at this moment.

"Darcy please," pleads Tate, his voice breaking. I let myself take another deep breath before opening my eyes, but he is no longer standing in front of me. He's fallen to his knees, his shoulders rising and falling aggressively as he bawls, "Please just talk to me. You don't have to forgive me today, tomorrow, or even next week. Please just have a conversation with me, my heart can't handle being iced out by you. I miss you just as much as I missed him. I love you more than I ever imagined was possible and it's eating me from the inside out that you can't look at me without disgust in your eyes."

My resolve is rapidly dwindling as I look down into his eyes, bearing witness to the pain trapped behind them, but something is still preventing me from giving in to him. I can't bring myself to say anything, just gently shaking my head and continuing down the hallway leaving Tatum and my heart behind on the kitchen floor.

Chapter 31

You Big Idiot

Tatum ‖ 6 weeks old, March

It's been three weeks since my world was shattered when I broke my family. Every day since my return to reality, I've been going and seeing Hayden and Darcy. She still won't speak to me. I've brought lilies and lasagna a few times, hoping Darcy will at least have a conversation with me over dinner but instead the lilies are thrown unwatered into a vase and the lasagna slid into the fridge.

Now I'm banging on my best friend's front door because he won't speak to me and I know Kodi and Bella aren't home because they are with my girl and my child. He's given me the silent treatment since I left Darcy and I can't blame him for ignoring me, I deserve it. I don't deserve any of my friends but almost all of them continue to reach out checking in on me... And standing by Darcy's.

When the door swings open, a red-faced Maverick appears and I hear a crunch before I feel it.

"Fuck!" I scream.

Barely able to process that Maverick just punched me in

the nose, blood trickles down my face and my eyes are watering so hard I can barely see.

"Get your ass in here, and sit the fuck down," Maverick orders. "You're going to listen and not say a fucking word because if you open your mouth, I will punch you again," Mav says, softer this time as he throws a black rag at my face for me to hold over my nose. Unwilling to be punched again, I just nod along as I nurse my still-leaking nose. "Why the fuck would you do that shit? You know what I went through with Bella, you witnessed me panic firsthand about whether Lily would just randomly show up and the struggles that come with being a single parent. Then that woman, *my* wife's best friend walks into your life and you run. Bolting without a word, and leaving us to all think we are going to do this all over again. You ran without even coming to me, Tate. I'm supposed to be your fucking best friend. I could've talked some sense into you. You can't seriously expect me to just be okay with this."

"Can I speak now?" I ask, it's muffled by the rag and angle of my head to stop the bleeding.

"Yes." His pacing has slowed but his arms remain crossed over his chest.

"You wouldn't have been able to talk sense into me, I was too deep in my head. I know that what I did was fucked up, I don't deserve any of you guys to forgive me. I don't deserve her, either. She's too kind and loving for me. She's too good for me."

"Well..." He huffs. "I could've knocked you out and stopped you from leaving at least. Dude you still don't believe that she will forgive you?"

"It's been weeks and I haven't gotten so much as four words or a smile from her. Most of the time my mom is at the condo and Darcy only comes into the room to feed

Hayden. The other day I got on my knees, begging her to talk to me and she just left me there."

"Are you putting in the work? Like truly." He's sitting now, the anger dissipating from the space.

"I'm showing up, Hayden smiles at me now but she still won't talk to me aside from a few words here and there. I've tried bringing her dinner and flowers, and while I know I can't buy her love, I was hoping at least to buy myself a conversation. I've been doing some reading too, trying to help myself become more in tune with my emotions and what to do when the self-doubt creeps in."

Harley recommended the books to me after swearing me to secrecy along with urging me to find a therapist. Harls is supposed to be mad at me but she knows that Darcy will appreciate that she did that someday. At Harls' suggestion, I've reached out to a few offices in the area and am waiting to get my first appointment scheduled. For now, the books Harley recommended will have to do.

"It's going to take more than some flowers and food to get her to talk to you."

"I just... I don't know what else to do."

"What have you not said to her that you think she needs to hear?" Maverick asks and I have to take a moment to think about it.

"I wish I could tell you, man. I feel like I cut my own chest open and spread my heart on the floor for her when I came back." I find myself rubbing my sternum, the pain from that day seeping back in.

"Do you think that maybe because the emotions were high, she didn't believe you meant it and instead assumed you were saying it because you wanted her to forgive you?"

"I don't know, Mav."

"I think maybe you should go to her, try and tell her

again. She might still need space but you can lay it out again. Just like she continued to tell you that you were enough, you can tell her that you will continue to fight for her, and fight for your family." Maverick's words sink in, and it isn't long before I'm thanking him and heading to the condo.

The elevator dings and I step out, coming face to face with Kodi and Bella.

"Bye, Uncle Tater Tot!" Bella waves rambunctiously beside Kodi.

"Don't fuck this up. She'll kill me if she finds out I told you this, but she loves you, you big buffoon." Kodi whispers, squeezing my arm gently and stepping into the elevator.

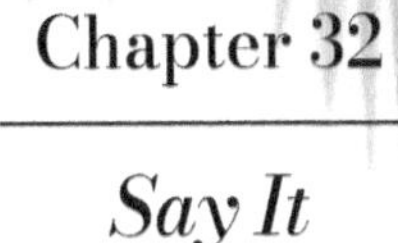

Chapter 32

Say It

Darcy ‖ 6 weeks old, March

"Darcy, you are my best friend and I am very rarely on anybody's side except yours," Kodi says and I brace myself for the truth bomb she is about to drop on me. I know exactly where this conversation is going—I've been moping for the past two weeks and I could very easily solve my own problems but I'm choosing to avoid them, too afraid to open myself to heartbreak.

"And yet it would appear that today you are not on mine," I sulk.

"You would be correct in assuming that."

"I really don't want to do this Ko."

Again. I know where this is going and if someone else tells me to talk to him, then I'll cave to my burning desire to hear him say he loves me and needs me again.

"Just hear me out." Her hands wringing in her lap tell me she's bracing herself for me to be angry with her.

"Out with it, I know exactly what you're going to say.

Hit me with the bestie bomb so I can finally come to my senses."

"I have never seen you so miserable in your life—not even when your parents made you end things with Kent. I know that what Tatum did was messed up but I also hate to tell you that you used to run too. When life got hard, when your parents were being extra controlling, when you got too close to a man, where did you run to?"

"The beach." Fucking hell, she's right.

"So what did Tatum do when life got hard, when his mind became too much?"

"Ran to the beach. This is different though Kodi, I didn't leave my partner and child behind."

"You're right. Again, I'll say that how he handled things wasn't the correct way. You are my best friend, you are in love with that man, and he is in love with you. While trust has to be rebuilt, it can't be if you won't even hear what he has to say." There it is, the thing I needed to hear straight from the one person who knows me better than anyone else.

"I'm scared." I pause, taking a deep breath, "I'm scared that if I hear him out, my resolve will break. That I'll let myself get wrapped up in him again in his love and kind words and gestures and then he will break me all over again."

"It's okay to be scared, the best things in life come from taking a chance when you're scared. Wouldn't you agree?" She nods her head in the direction of Bella lying with her head on the outside of Hayden's baby tot watching Lion King as he sleeps, his little hand wrapped around her thumb.

"I guess I do. I'll talk to him. I think he's coming over today."

"Yep, should be on the elevator..." She glances at her

phone, "Now actually. Bella baby, it's time to go see Daddy."

Kodi and I stand, and I wrap my arms around her, "thank you Kodi. For everything, love ya."

"Love ya."

A few minutes later I'm pacing the living room, Hayden transferred to his crib and when Tatum crosses the threshold, my body tingles in his presence. His mouth opens and closes a few times but words fail him.

"Let's sit outside?" I offer, hoping that transitioning out of this area will help him gather his thoughts. I can't be the one to start this conversation because he needs to get out his thoughts first. He nods his head and follows me to the patio, I sit facing inward first bringing my legs beneath me then patting the cushion next to me, giving him the permission he needs to be in close proximity with me.

"Darcy."

"Tatum." I quirk a brow at him, waiting but not pushing him to speak until he feels ready.

"I know that I've said this more times than you can count but I'm going to tell you again that I'm sorry."

"Thank you." I have to give him something, starting with acknowledging an apology he's tried to give over and over again.

"It's not okay, none of it was okay." He sucks in a deep breath, his frustration and sadness palpable between us.

"I know it wasn't okay but I'm telling you that I accept your apology." I give him an encouraging nod and find myself reaching for his hands, his engulf mine but I want him to know I'm here and I'm listening.

"Thank you." A tear slips free from his eye. "You and Hayden mean everything to me; you both are my world. I tore that apart and there's been a gaping hole in my heart where you both belong. I want," He starts, before shaking his head, "no, I need you both back in my life. I can't express to you how sorry I am. I can't tell you enough that I love you but I'm going to try. These past two weeks have been my rock bottom and I will do whatever it takes to bring us back together."

"It might take me some time to fully trust you again or to not clam up when I feel like you're pulling away. I think we need to communicate better though. When it's hard, when we need to tap out, or when we need more from the other person." His grip on my hand tightens as I speak, a quick glimmer of hope passing over his eyes.

"Ma-" He stops himself but I find myself vehemently shaking my head then pressing my forehead to his.

"Say it."

"Mama, tell me that means what I think it means."

I don't say anything, I instead crawl into his lap, straddling him in broad daylight, wrapping my hands around the back of his neck and pulling his lips to mine in a desperate clashing of tongues and teeth.

Tatum pulls back first, panting, "I promise you that I will never do that again. I've been self reflecting, I'm trying to do better. I need you in my life Darcy, I can't do life without you. I love you."

"I love you."

"Fuck, I missed hearing you say that." He brings his lips to mine again but it's cut short by Hayden's small cries coming through my phone.

Epilogue- Vitamin You

Gathered at the beach house, surrounded by our loved ones, my hands are shaking violently in my pockets around the little velvet box I've been carrying around all day.

"Ready for this?" Nik's strong hand comes down on my shoulder as we watch Hayden waddle at high speed around the living room with Bella.

"Ready as I'll ever be. I gotta go get him changed." Proposing here by the beach seemed like the best fit, in our happy place celebrating our son's first birthday with all of our favorite people. I go and scoop Hayden up, "Alright little man outfit change time."

Darcy catches me as I'm headed to Hayden's nursery and I almost spit it out at the way she looks up at me, eyes wide, lips parted and baby blue dress clinging to her chest perfectly.

"Where are my two favorite guys headed?"

"Was just going to change his diaper and then figured

we could do the cake since he would already be naked." I smile down at her.

"Are you okay? Do you not feel well, you're pale?" She asks, her eyebrows knitted in concern.

"All good Mama, in need of a little vitamin you is all."

"Daddy," her voice quiet, face heated, "you shouldn't say that out loud."

"I mean it, be right back. Love you." I quickly kiss her then send her across the room giving Kodi the *it's time* wink behind Darcy's head. I dash to Hayden's nursery, pulling out the t-shirt I had made specially for today and changing his diaper.

When we return to the kitchen, Kodi has Darcy facing the other way and everyone is gathered under the guise that they are about to sing Happy Birthday. I set Hayden down and whisper, "Go show Mommy your new shirt buddy." Already a team player, he beelines it for Darcy, trying to go around to her back before Kodi easily redirects him. Kodi steps out of the way as Hayden pulls on the end of D's dress.

She scoops him up. "Hey bud, I thought you were supposed t-" She stops dead in her tracks as she reads his shirt that says 'Marry my daddy?' and I drop to one knee behind her. Eyes widen around the room and breaths are held in anticipation of what's to come.

"Mama?" My hands shaking already and when she turns to me, tears are welling in her eyes.

"Darcy, you and Hayden have been the highlight of my life. The joy you've brought into my life over the past two years is more than I thought I would ever be blessed enough to experience in my lifetime. I've been lucky enough to be surrounded by your love and light— then when I got a mini version of you, well, I was done for. Marry me?" I pull the box out of my pocket, where a moss agate hexagon cut ring sits on a plush bed of velvet.

"YES! Oh my God, yes please!" She jumps a few times, and Hayden giggles thinking she's playing with him. I place the ring on her finger and then stand pulling her into me for a kiss, Hayden squirms on her hip done with us.

"One second, buddy. Mommy and Daddy just need some pictures then you can go play." I smile down at him, he's a spitting image of Darcy but his hair and skin tone are more akin to mine. I wonder what our next child will look like.

"Oh my God!" I hear a cacophony of squeals come from the general direction of Darcy's best friend. I'm honestly surprised Kodi didn't spill the beans to the others. Mav, Dom, Collins, and Nik are wiping away tears. My best friends are tough but one thing that always gets them is love. I hear sniffles coming from my Mom and I see the twins' mime gagging out of the corner of my eye.

"What do you think of the ring?" I ask Darcy as she sits beside me, the buzz of the party beginning to slow down.

"It's everything I've ever wanted. Kodi gave you the ideas?" She asks, holding her left hand up and taking in the ring again.

"Yes, but I also pay attention, you've mentioned what you were wanting in a ring to me," I smirk.

"Well it's beautiful. Thank you, Tate, I can't wait to marry you." She leans in, kissing me again, and fuck I can't wait for this party to be over.

"You look so fucking pretty with only a ring on." I groan as I push myself into Darcy, slowly but not fast enough for her, already down on all fours and spread open for me. Her ring glistens in the moonlight streaming through the window of our beach house bedroom.

"Daddy, please." She pushes her ass against me, seeking more. Fuck me, I love when she calls me Daddy, but I don't want to rush tonight.

I want to enjoy my fiancé.

"Please what Mama?"

"Give me your cock, I need it so badly." She's not lying, I'm barely halfway in and she's strangling me already.

"Since you asked so nicely." I push myself in, filling her all the way but remaining still. Her moans echo throughout the room. I begin to thrust in and out of her, letting my hand roam up and grasp the back of her neck and hold her in place. When her legs begin to shake and her moans crescendo, I snake a hand to her front, pinching her clit and tossing her over the edge. As her body writhes beneath mine, I welcome the telltale tingle at the base of my spine. She reaches back, massaging my balls, and I explode into her with a roar.

Extended Epilogue- Pretty Pink Stain

Throughout the past eight years with Tatum, life has been a dream. We married, I've released five full-length novels with a sixth on the way, my parents are around but at a far enough distance to maintain my sanity and Tate kept his promise to breed me over and over again resulting in us having three more children since Hayden. Quincy came when Hayden was still a toddler, Calliope took a little longer to conceive but she and Teddy are thick as thieves- Ko and I are secretly hoping they fall in love. Juni —our little surprise joined us six months ago and we are having our first kid-free night in almost a year.

To say I'm excited is an understatement. Uninterrupted time with my hunky husband and uninterrupted sleep is going to be a dream. *Thank you, Walter and Rose.*

I'm standing in the bathroom of the beach house, the place we now permanently call home, touching up my makeup when I see Tatum approach. He crosses his arms, leaning on the doorframe as he waits for me to finish spreading my lipstick. Eight years, and I still get butterflies when he looks at me this way.

"Happy anniversary." I smile at him through my reflection.

"Happy anniversary. You know I'm going to wipe that pretty pink stain off of your lips with my cock tonight, right?"

"I was betting on it..." I turn on my heel, pressing into his chest and leaning into his ear as I exit, "Daddy." And fucking hell I'm already dripping for him.

I don't make it far before he's got my wrists pinned above my head and my back pressed to the wall, his erection hard against my thigh. "Don't tease me, Mama." His hot breath fans against my neck as he rubs his nose along my jaw, "I planned a whole date for us and if you keep it up we won't make it there."

"What if I'd rather do this instead?" I quickly turn my lips to his, nipping at his lower one and pushing my hips forward.

"Trust me there will be plenty of this later and it's going to be worth the wait." He groans letting his lips find mine for a few more moments before basically dragging me out of the house and to our date.

AFTER THE BEST lobster risotto I've ever had and almost an entire bottle of white wine, we make it back to the house and all I can think about is my husband's cock. His hand posessively held my thigh the whole drive and it had me squirming beneath his grip. Now I sit on the edge of the bed as he, at a painfully slow speed, undoes the buttons on his crisp white shirt.

"Could you go any slower?" I jest, knowing that if I get him riled up, I'll have him sooner.

"Mm, actually I could." He somehow begins to move slower, fine I can play dirty too. We've been together for long enough that you'd think we've tried everything and we probably have tried a lot but if there's one surefire thing to get my husband to hustle, it's if I touch myself.

I stand, pulling my purple sweater dress over my head revealing the new black and lacy lingerie the girls helped me pick out. His movement stalls, drinking in my body—the way my chest heaves, the crotchless panties that give him easy access, and my taught nipples beneath the lace. Without missing a beat, I lower myself back to the bed, lifting my feet and spreading myself wide. I trail a pointed nail down the middle of my chest and tease over each nipple slowly.

"Darcy, what are you doing?" He growls, unbuttoning a little quicker. I continue the perusal of my own body, stopping just at my clit, not touching just hovering.

"Nothing." I moan, dragging a finger down my slit and back up circling my bundle of nerves.

"Why are you playing without me?"

"Taking too long." I continue to circle my clit, my eyes closing and my head slowly dropping back as pleasure begins to fuel my movements. My hand is ripped away and then Tatum's mouth is latched onto my pussy. *Bingo.*

"Oh fuck." I let my hand slide into his hair, my hips bucking into his face.

"Couldn't wait for me?" He breathes over my wetness, sending a chill through my body.

"Just had to get you where I wanted." He doesn't get a chance to respond because my grip on his hair tightens and I push his mouth back onto me. He eats me like a man starved and if you ask him, he has been for the past almost ten months. It doesn't take long before my vision is blurring and my body is trembling as Tatum's name belts from my lips.

"Turn, head off the bed." He demands once I've ridden out my orgasm.

"Yes, Daddy." I open my mouth, relax my jaw, and wait. Tate taps his cock on my tongue a few times, caressing my cheek as he looks down at me.

"I told you I was going to ruin this pretty pink stain." And he does.

About the Author

Katelyn is a Florida native, born and raised. She lives with her husband, Adam and their two dogs, Yogi the goldendood and Smoosh the pocket pittie mix. She's not a fan of being outdoors but enjoys the occasional excursion to the mountains, hoping to one day experience life there. Returning to her love of reading when the COVID pandemic struck, she rediscovered she's a fan of all genres and all things spicy. She gravitates most towards hockey romances while ironically enough she isn't a follower of hockey. Her writing is a labor of love outside of her full time Nanny job to the cutest two under two. If she's not reading or writing, you can find her playing cozy games on the Nintendo switch, in a Dungeons & Dragons campaign, or binge watching bad reality TV.

Acknowledgments

I published my second book, like hello?? To publish one book was a feat for me but to publish two in seven months like wowee!

Now onto the people that helped me get here in no particular order.

To my critique partner, Mindy Pettengill. Mindy, as always your feral reactions and valuable feedback helped to turn On Three... Baby Reed into the story that I envisioned. You also helped me with promotion, hyping up my posts, bringing my art to life and being an all around support system since our goldfish brains get along so well. Thank you putting up with my nonsense everyday and being a best friend- the Devil couldn't find me so he put you across the country.

To my alphas, Kris, Jensen, and Ryan. Thank you all for your excitement as you read On Three... Baby Reed! You each brought incredible feedback and incredible social media content that had me laughing out loud.

To my betas, Allison, Bailey, Chachi, Cierra, and Jessie. Thank you for taking the time to beta read for me, your feedback specifically on pregnancy has been so helpful in shaping Darcy and Tatum's journey.

To Harley, my PA. You may have come into the On Three... Baby Reed journey towards the end but your help with graphics and brainstorming has already been so helpful! I'm excited to grow with you by my side.

To my parents, I'm sorry that you can't read this book either even though I know you'll have a signed copy on your shelf I can't thank you enough for your love and support my whole life, like when I decided to play softball or joined the winterguard team with no athletic ability you encouraged me to practice and grow everyday. That encouragement is what led me to finish my second book and publish it knowing you would be proud of me.

To Adam, my husband, the sunshine to my grumpy and my knight in shining tin foil. When I looked at you and said I'm writing another book, you encouraged me to do so seeing how much joy it brought me to write Shot to the Hart. When I was stressing again over deadlines, costs of services and about actually publishing for people to see my book with their eyeballs, you continued to tell me how proud of me you were and that no matter what people thought, I did it and I should be proud of that too. I love you so many.

To my real life Darcy, aka Em. I'm sorry that I wrote your character as pregnant, I know this is not in the cards for you but I had to haha. Half of our lives and you still give me unconditional support and I couldn't do it without you.

To Carly. Thank you for designing my stickers, I love them all.

To my Chaos Crew, thank you all for sharing, liking, and reposting. For letting me bounce ideas off of you, for hyping me and both my book babies up before they was even in your hands,

for deciding where spicy scenes should take place and helping expand the book playlist. You all are amazing!

Lastly to my readers, this is my second book and if you've read it well I can't thank you enough. I didn't think people would be excited about my first book, let alone my second but there were more people than I could imagine who wanted to meet my characters and you being one of them just makes my day! I hope you stick around for what's next in the Scoring with Love series.